AF243936

# The Well-Loved Demon

NATACHA PAVLOV

*The Well-Loved Demon* is a work of historical fiction. Any references to historical events, real people, or real places are used fictitiously. Any other events are products of the author's imagination, and any resemblance to actual events, places or living persons is entirely coincidental.

Copyright © 2022 by Natacha Pavlov
All rights reserved.
No portion of this book may be reproduced in any form without written permission from the author, except as permitted by U.S. copyright law. Please refer all pertinent questions to the author-publisher at www.natachapavlov.com.

First paperback edition, 2022.
Printed in the United States of America.

Cover art design by Welder Wings for © Natacha Pavlov. Based on the original painting portrait of Louis XV by Maurice Quentin de La Tour, 1748.

Bible scripture from THE HOLY BIBLE, NEW INTERNATIONAL VERSION®, NIV® Copyright © 1973, 1978, 1984, 2011 by Biblica, Inc.™ Used by permission. All rights reserved worldwide.

ISBN – 978-0-9966928-4-7

These people honor me with their lips,
but their hearts are far from me.
They worship me in vain;
their teachings are merely human rules.
(Matthew 15:8-9)

*It will be known that King Louis XV of the illustrious House of Bourbon is as much a powerful king as a boldly artistic man of letters. And what better way than to display it in the inferior, plain English language of his bitterest enemy? Better for the common masses to hear him and know they are not, and will never be, out of his great hunter's reach.*

*If truth be told, he has not intended anyone to see his penned memoirs except his closest. Yet who can be closest to him than himself? As little as a king needs to justify his actions, it is another token of his goodness that he has offered the world of letters the bittersweet gift of his inmost royal thoughts.*

It is always spring in that other perfect place out of my reach.

Spring bursting with bergamot and lavender; raining with sparkling *vin de Champagne* and our endless *Louis d'or* coins and floating banknotes; materializing, pouring in like golden fountains... but mostly evaporating into thin air. Spring: blinding with my beloved Brillant's heavenly white Angora fur... and then the feathers and hairy flesh reeking of iron-scented crimson.

The Great Chain of Being. It's for that holy order of hierarchy and our divine right: from God, through angels, humans, animals, plants, to minerals. Isn't it? Our forests of Compiègne, Fontainebleau, Choisy, Rambouillet, Saint-Hubert, Bellevue, and la Muette, among others, require our perpetual royal presence and display of power. A king learns to think and say such things without showing emotion. The betrayal of such could arm an enemy, after all.

On my darker days, I'll secretly think of myself as Saturn, reaping the bountiful flesh to fill our feasts, the undeniable proof of our constant harvest to glorify my rule. If only it could always be this easy: to simply soar through forested time and grasp my desired prey, shedding and renewing myself with each new carcass to benefit my subjects.

There is a truth—so why my lingering restlessness? Would constant happiness and satisfaction automatically prove my sound judgment? Why born to err so much—but I stop myself, for if God wants us living and dying, we cannot go against His will. The philosophers will ask and answer such things, to varying degrees of satisfaction.

Though I was born into power, I was left to my own devices at the tender age of two; my parents and older brother abandoning me to my orphaned fate. History will remember the date of October 25, 1722 as the one I was crowned at Reims. Subleyras's skilled brush shows the twelve-year-old pious king I am, kneeling with my joined hands in my scarlet ensemble.

Perhaps it is fitting that my crown wasn't painted in, for it was not a crown I wanted, though I dared not say it aloud. I felt its weight, and not just from its dazzling Sancy diamond, the Regent diamond, and other precious stones and pearls. Clovis I, Charlemagne, the canonized Louis IX, and most of all, my intimidating great-grandfather Louis XIV looked down on me with the glory of their eternal success. Yet even at that young age I knew that I was angel, demon, human, and animal; encompassing the entire chain. If I'd expressed my rejection of the worldly crown, would I have been considered the era's first philosopher-king, in my appearance of pure, youthful simplicity?

I wanted to run, far and away—from the blood, from men's groans under my window, from my nightmares that robbed me of rest, from Cardinal Fleury and his damning sermons, from marriage and women's pettiness that *maman* Ventadour so blessedly lacked. I wanted to run to the forest where the wildlife roamed, and be free like a French noble savage that I was—and still am. Despite my age and delicate constitution, I was a healthy man; my beloved, trusted surgeon Mareschal could testify to that, after all.

But I couldn't escape.

Trapped, I remained in my torturous cycle of anxiety, pleasure, and revenge that I both love and hate. Strangely in my torment I seize an odd thrill to think that my crown, this curious symbol of my rule, would survive the ages well after I'd gone. If it was then that I first learned to wear several masks, I was only following example.

In those early years of the Regent Phillipe II, Duc d'Orléans ruling in my place, I tried to seek out a sense of happiness in being back at my birthplace of Versailles, where Louis XIV had reigned and died. Out of respect for his memory, I resolved to keep the place mostly as he'd built it, and I submitted to the daily *lever* and *coucher* ceremonies in his sacred frigid bedroom that had become mine that made for tedious, yet familiar custom.

I tried to imagine my mother, Marie Adélaïde, the Duchess of Burgundy's movements about the place, and stifled my sad jealousy that Louis XIV had so enjoyed her presence that she was one of the rare adored women of his life. Sometimes I'd stare hard, my eye sockets so still that I thought they'd freeze into place, hoping I wouldn't miss it when she might appear and grant me her motherly love I yearned for.

Other times I longed for my earlier years at the Tuileries where in the care of my beloved governess Madame de Ventadour—my angelic *maman* who saved me from death at the hands of incompetent doctors—I did not follow the strict protocol. Then again, at seven I'd been ripped from her care by the Duc de Villeroy, who deplorably taught me court etiquette and the duties of my crown, and forced me to perform in two ballets. My terror—those evil eyes, mixed with greed and amusement, all fixed on me with their endless demands—had morphed into rage and resolve that never again would I be forced, let alone dictated how to act for entertainment.

Still, in those moments when I felt alone, worried, or afraid, I took to thinking of Rigaud's painting of me from then, where he made me look older and majestic in the royal white, blue, and gold regalia of my forebears. In it, my posture evokes Louis XIV, with the scepter of rule in my right hand, and the insignia of the Order of the Holy Spirit on my chest. Naturally, there's also the French royal crown and the sword of Charlemagne. At first I'd been confused and annoyed by this depiction, when everyone knew I didn't yet look like that. A sense of inferiority and hurry overcame me to match its appearance, until I gradually considered that it might not be impossible, and even pleasant, to let it inspire me with its sanctioned deception.

Immersed in Versailles, I roamed the halls in my Saturnian melancholy, the clashes of ancestral battles echoing in my soul. At the *Salon de Guerre* I'd admire the bas-relief of my great-grandfather, wishing I could crush my enemies on horseback as confidently as he did, and with Clio, the muse of history at his feet, to likewise sing my praises. I wanted that same majesty, that lasting representation of power that would allow me to rule successfully while also obeying his last advice not to make war as much as he had.

Though I doubted my own role among the monarchs, I often gazed up at the sky, searching as much for marvel and escape as for guiding answers. Such was that late May day of '24, when at the Trianon gardens with Jacques Cassini—whose father Giovanni had begun a map of France—and the whole court, I watched the sun darken in total eclipse. Some said they were omens of the end of the world, and as I wondered if it held clues to my future, the alternating light and darkness only added to my warring fearful confusion and rebellious indifference tinged with defiance.

Often when I least expected it, the thought of the devastating plague of Marseille that had struck but a few years before stabbed my core. I dreaded the hellish image of mountains of maggot-infested corpses, gnawed on by rats, cats, dogs, and other starved animals... and worst of all, dying without absolution—for they surely couldn't all have been attended to in time as death swept through. Sometimes I shook off the sadness by thinking of the Chevalier de Roze's heroic work, and in the spirit of continuation, I thought it fitting to resume the work on the *Salon d'Hercule*, left unfinished at Louis XIV's death.

I liked to immerse myself in studies of history, geography, and botany, and the art of wood, silver, and ivory lathe turning. I loved when in my focus I'd enter mysterious, yet peaceful other realms. But too often, something seemed to lurk around me, eager to tarnish and shorten my comfort. It reminded me of the poetic passage in the epic novel *L'Astrée*, where Celion compares his unrest to an eternal fountain.

There was one solace to my aimless unrest, and that was hunting; the one thing I could do without boredom or exhaustion. I treasured my stables full of horses, and my greyhound and spaniel hunting dogs so important to our excursions, and to provide me with as many antlers as possible to decorate my Stags' Courtyard. Likewise I loved the Chevalier de Beringhen as much for being one of my favorite hunting companions, as for introducing me to the artist Jean-Baptiste Oudry who specialized in still-life and hunting scenes. I was too pleased to soon commission him to paint my two favorite greyhounds, Misse and Turlu.

And yet, a tormenting thought presented itself to me. Could a painting ever truly capture the distress of the hunt? The rush of the chase consumed me: flying in the wind with Diana, twin of Apollo, at my side, as I charged after my prey that I never failed to swiftly catch. Drifting on the power of sound guidance, conquering the darkness; what else could be more important to a hopeful young king? In the fifteenth century, Jeanne the Maiden had first heard her voices in a garden that led her to defy the English; I could only hope this was my own sacred version of it.

The black eyes—alert, defiant, then terrified—demanding I impale deep into them their final frozen expression. I hated the torturous build-up named *wait*, when I'd waited long enough. Strangely, time stood still as the air thickened, slowly suffocating... until the chaotic hunting horn and wailing symphony of the kill—that only I, the king, had the right to make! The ritual went on, filling my ears with the sound of pumping blood as the testicles were first cut—and set aside for my own potential savoring—while the warm viscera and hearts were ripped out and fed to the restless dogs as fitting rewards.

But it always ended with the misshapen antlers, contorting and reaching every which way, splattered with blood and ever pointing back at me. I wasn't sure about the Devil's horns and hooves, but I took a twisted delight in thinking that, had he morphed as deceivers are bound to do, each time I robbed it of its temporary earthly receptacle. I'd learned to shoot before I wore the crown, so it was no fault of mine if it became my first and most loyal love, and when by comparison, so much else seemed nearly pointless.

I was a young bored lonely king, and in my reluctance of girls and women—and worse, of the venereal sicknesses they brought—there was no shortage of courtiers young and old to please me. Not because I wanted them to, but because in their hope to rise above their lower ranks they vainly thought they could seduce me; show me things, teach me and enlighten me with pleasures unknown. As if it was them doing it by their own mighty talents rather than vilest witchcraft, when it was I the chosen monarch, granted great sacred might. Perhaps their minds were corrupted by the ancient Roman-Italian vice—hoping to strengthen their manly-warrior bond—or fueled by the libertine Regent Philippe d'Orléans, whose father Philippe I was famous for the vice.

As the Venetians surely know—whose coveted mirrors adorn our Hall of Mirrors—there's power in masks, as there are in secrets; in not revealing everything to others, when a friend can so easily become foe, or even an inadvertent pawn in someone else's schemes. One of my early secret discoveries was finding that some tastes and inclinations can be imposed on us, but only with our continued participation.

As such, as a lonely orphaned young man having no preference, and even disgust for both of these strange creations, I didn't know what to choose. But having no preference does not mean desire for the first given encounter, or desire for both, or even any. It simply remains that it came first and whether or not it holds is revealed in due time. While legion are my vices, and that Mareschal's and Fleury's warning guidance were indispensable, that is one I valiantly cast into the flames early on, and can only be done by one's committed rejection.

In further searching myself, I knew that it was right to keep myself as pure as I could for my eventual wife, and not soil myself with other women, just as I would have the same from her. Nor did I lack some discernment when, besides *maman*, there were women I cared for; namely my cousin Mademoiselle de Charolais, said to be the most beautiful Princess of the House of Bourbon, and Marie Victoire Sophie de Noailles, Countess of Toulouse. Of this dear countess's château in Rambouillet I preserve the fondest memories, where the strict etiquette of Versailles vanished in favor of true friendship and liberty amidst an intimate circle. In this aura of quieter retreat, Mademoiselle de Charolais brought her libertine ways and flair for the boisterous that she tempered for the countess's contrasting pious nature. I often felt that there I could shed my cold mask for something gentler, and I hoped, truer to my nature.

My initial idea of marriage was revolting and paralyzing when presented with the four-year old Infanta Mariana Victoria of Spain. Organized by the Regent to reconcile France with Spain after years of war, he had not even taken care to ask me, but rather to inform me of it with a hint of finality. A coiled rage rose up in me—disgusting, but oh so enthralling, addicting! If they did not consult me for my feelings, and for such an important matter as the one I'd share the future of the empire with, then what else were they conspiring against me? Surely I could have them all answer for this, in a range of ways...

The battle raged, forcing my tears, but I froze—what else could I do but surrender? Did it really matter to me one way or another? So I sealed my lips and kept my innermost thoughts from them, as they did with me. All I could do was relish their toil in trying to get me to utter a word, but I said nothing.

Alone I fumed, the angry and frustrated twelve-year old boy wishing only for his *maman* Ventadour. From the moment the Infanta arrived, and through her three years at court, I wanted nothing else but to ignore her, as captivated as she was by my person.

She met with great favor and the Princess Palatine fawned over her wit, beauty, and maturity, but I saw through it. There had to be something unnatural in such a young girl to resist sound counsel and being bled when faced with feverous measles. How she refused to offer her arm to the wise Mareschal—and while residing in the apartments where my own mother had died of the very disease eleven years prior! The Infanta fussed and folded her arms over herself, refusing to be intimidated by the doctors and ruses meant to finally get her to acquiesce, as if she saw through them and surpassed their knowledge. It took an officer and four armed bodyguards posted near her bed that she believed were sent by my command for her to surrender to the procedure. Even afterwards she had the pride to vaunt her bravery to *maman*—using the same title for her that I did; perhaps the only thing we had in common. For his skill and trouble I awarded Mareschal the Order of Saint Michael for successfully treating her.

In what had to be divine intervention the Regent died; ending an increasingly impopular rule that had caused much grief with his support of John Law's disastrous bank and paper currency reforms and its dreams of overnight wealth. As such, the marriage arrangement came to an end—she was simply too young and I could not be kept unmarried and without an heir for so long, and risk the throne going to the House of Orléans, they said. So off she went on an unsuspecting carriage ride back to Spain while I was at Marly, continuing my life without her.

The future of France always looming over us, the question of my wedding persisted. From over a hundred princesses was chosen the humble Polish Princess Marie Leczinska. During the Great Northern War, her father Stanislas I had usurped the throne with Swedish support, only to be soon overthrown. With her twenty-two years to my fifteen, it assured everyone that I would be shortly with an heir. She was not what they called beautiful but I saw something familiar and comforting in her shy and pious demeanor.

It may have been my duty, and yet I welcomed the growing hope that the prospect of our wedding seemed to bring to my erratic, moody heart. Finally I would be blessed to enjoy the carnal pleasure sanctioned by the church to be fruitful and prosper. Cardinal Fleury cautioned me on the serious nature of the duty, even as I was shown illicit sculptures and other scenes of the patriarchs in the procreative act, none of which made it more appealing. Decidedly, it was a mystery that I would have to discover myself and which no one else could understand except the Queen and I.

I will be unashamedly sentimental in saying our wedding was a dream. Like the Queen, I imagined only one such lavish affair in my life, so I wanted it to be a heavenly vision and wallowed in all the joy and sense of accomplishment it brought. The *Te Deum* hymn blessed our union, we had our great feast, and—with our ambassador to Venice Jacques-Vincent Languet's suggestion—the commissioned

Vivaldi serenata *Gloria e Imeneo*. There was also Molière's plays *Amphitryon* and *Le Médecin malgré lui*, to our collective great enjoyment.

When at last we were alone in our bed, we mirrored pinched smiles and shy awkwardness. The Queen gently offered caresses and I went along with it, reminding myself that not only was it allowed to take it all the way to the end, but blessed by our Catholic faith.

But I couldn't.

I fidgeted, sweaty like a baby ready to wet the bed. I'd said no before, long before her, wanting to be strong and invincible, and yet weak and ashamed before this burgeoning inner hunger that frightened me, even as it was said to make me a man. I'd said no, but he'd kept going as if he enjoyed my confused, tormented longing. Trapped—was that all I would ever be?

The Queen saw my reluctance, and in her affectionate piety she was so soft and gentle that I could try to see us both as innocent children, just trying to do what we were told. Gradually I relaxed enough to let her keep caressing me and guided her hand down to the familiar motion. Though I read her flush of reluctant confusion, she meekly acquiesced to my satisfaction. I quickly kissed her cheek and rolled over, before she could see the tears in my eyes or demand more than I could give that first night.

I couldn't tell her, and sensed that I never could utter to such a pious creature how afraid I'd been, yet how relieved I was that it was so different—so unlike men's groans, men's hardness and animalistic pheromones... In my limited experience I didn't know much, nor did I want to think of it then, or at any time—but it was enough to confirm that I'd gotten out of that unnatural grasp. I decided that I'd publicly announce that we'd crowned our union seven times, which she naturally wouldn't contradict or even confirm regarding our intimacies.

As time passed she tried to submissively guide me over her, but even dazed with Champagne—that blessed drink I first tasted at my coronation—I couldn't yet, let alone say when it would finally happen. That any delay in pregnancy was usually blamed on the woman afforded me some time, at least.

Amidst our burgeoning union we had an excuse to postpone our duty when came a delegation that soon had all France's attention. Our colony of Louisiana—though impressively encompassing most of the Mississippi River basin—had an uninteresting, and worse, bad reputation to the French subjects. To counter constant English and Spanish pressure, we needed our Indian allies to peacefully live along-side with and maintain trading with the French settlers. As such, it was our mission to show the five visiting Indians—four leaders and one daughter of a Chief—the might of the French to ensure our alliance.

Given their high standing, I received them along with other promi-nent members of the court, like my Prime Minister the Duc de Bour-bon, and the Duc d'Orléans, who was my heir should I die without a male heir.

I welcomed the contrast there was from the Turkish embassy four years before. Thankfully, my robust fifteen-year old frame might dis-simulate my lingering shyness, and perhaps even add a seriousness that might suggest a growing confidence I lacked as an eleven-year old. What a blessing that Villeroy wasn't there to display me like a gold-en-haired curiosity who'd turn, walk, and run at his vile command!

Unlike the unbelieving Turkish embassy, who'd come to glean knowledge from our great advancements, the Indians seemed to have no pretenses, and no wish to be like us or outdo us, even should they convert to our faith. I couldn't help but feel at ease with these visitors who seemed imbued with a deep inner strength coupled with an endearing innocence. I spent over an hour with our new guests, musing that the very walls of Versailles might absorb at least some of their powerful exotic essence.

Their chiseled bodies were sleek and tough, adorned in colorful drawings, jewelry, and feathers. A belt held up a loincloth at their waist, and they carried a bow and arrow, as if ever-ready for a fruitful hunt. They were pillars of strength; they who led simple lives in the heart of nature, and who'd fearlessly crossed the deadly Atlantic Ocean whose monstrous, nearly vertical walls of waves and mysterious whirlpools swallowed up unlucky travelers, never to be seen or heard from again. I knew right then that the Queen's wish to see them would be denied, for it was as unnecessary for her as it was inappropriate. Accompanied by my confessor Reverend Father Linières, she could well make do with meeting with the Jesuit Father de Beaubois to hear of his missionary work there.

The Indians were taken to see the sights of Paris, where they marveled at the roasting spits of the Hôtel des Invalides and the vast quantities of meat. But they seemed most amazed at the performance of the Opéra, and clapped to their delight, wishing to see the same thing the next day. At Marly they visited the royal apartments, the gardens, and fawned at the fountains whose animals spit water from invisible pipes.

They saw the Company of the Indies headquarters on several occasions, and in late November I wished to divert them on a hare hunt. As we flew amongst the trees, I imagined we were in that far-off land claimed by my great-grandfather, transforming me as they'd been transformed by the arrival of the French. I wondered what Louis XIV would say if he saw us hunting thus, and hoped that it would please him.

My blood pounded through my veins, and before I could stop myself, I mused: what if I, parentless, had been taken by such men and grown up with them? There'd be no court, no etiquette, and with a man's freedom, I'd be able to do as I wished with little need for explanation. Was it wrong, a betrayal to my own, to think that these men didn't seem to want anything from me, let alone wish to take my crown for themselves and rule in my place? And yet I'd heard the tales of their scalping victims as proof of prowess in the field. I vacillated between them surely mocking me if I couldn't do it, or winning their admiration if, in my greed, I outdid all of them.

As their departure approached, they were granted all the entertainments of the court and I offered them gifts worthy of their honorable stations: the royal medallion on a gold chain, a rifle, a game-bag, a sword, a watch, and a painting of the audience they'd had with me. The *Mercure de France* fed accounts to readers eager for exotic details of these foreigners, fueled by their recent shift from reading novels to travel accounts.

I said I'd always keep their Nation and its Chiefs in mind, and I hoped that they would speak kindly of us back in New Orleans and across the vast territory. Less pleasant was Montesquieu's *Lettres Persanes* in my mind, whose satirical portrait of Paris also included a new spirit of disrespect towards authority. Though I understood the veiled critique of the Regent and John Law that had led to inflation and bankruptcy, I forced myself—with the help of sparkling-gold Champagne—to think that this was all in the past, and would not repeat with sound government.

Providence seemed destined to remind me that the wild ever lurked when soon after we heard the news of a wild boy named Peter from Hanover. He'd been found in the forest by King George I's party of hunters during one of his visits. Where had he come from, and were there more of them? The hunger grew in me, too, and sometimes my gluttonous eating and drinking helped. Often it didn't.

I fled to my trusted Cardinal Fleury—whom I'd newly-appointed as Prime Minister—who tamed my excesses with his harsh words, he who claimed to be so above any earthly yearnings. Naturally I had to keep visiting the Queen's bed, and while I'd feigned my burning lust for her lest he—and the court—think me incapable of reproducing, I secretly asked for forgiveness and gave thanks that it was becoming more truthful by the moment. I easily agreed to temper myself and not touch the Queen who, despite her yearning empty womb, did not harass me. She clutched her rosary in ardent prayer and I hoped it would serve to add strength to our endeavor when the time finally came. What was I waiting for? I sipped the Champagne, shuddering as I realized it would be the ideal way to poison me if one wanted to.

At last, a fall night during the glorious hunting season, the urge won me over, and I fell over the Queen. Should she see the scar on my chest, I hoped she'd view it as a favorable sign of my survival from the antidote I'd been given as a gravely ill eleven-year old, and which spared me my parents' and brother's fate. As we gradually both struggled to control our panting, I wavered between wanting her not to see it, and her caressing it, maybe even sinking her teeth deep into it.

Curiously, in my frenzied pleasurable daze I saw Elizabeth, that daughter of Tsar Peter the Great, who'd been one of my many contenders. Was she gentle or robust like her father who'd swept me up in his arms eight years earlier during his visit to Versailles? Before I could stop it, I envisioned her in Russian costumes and furs, smelling of wild Russian Orthodox incense; so different from my Queen who lay beneath me, her eyes nearly pinched shut and wincing as I went harder, as if refusing to contest my growing violence... I thought of asking the Queen if she liked it, this consuming savage build up, but didn't want to unsettle her piety in forcing such a confession.

From that moment I wondered how I could've ever doubted the power of matrimony. It was everything, and better than what they said. My Queen could do no wrong, and I couldn't get enough of her feeding my growing husbandly hunger. And yet, once more, Cardinal Fleury had to reign in my enthusiasm when I'd just begun to taste its joys. Women are deceiving; the act is for procreation, not lust; a king has other affairs to tend to... But I only wanted to tend to her, if only until we were sure she was with child. What was a king if I would never have freedom to enjoy my wife as I pleased? At last I had my companion with whom I could enjoy my quiet intimate time; playing with our cats, reading Autreau's play *La Fille Inquiète*, Molière, or some maxims, or listen to her rave about her favorite dishes, desserts, or composers she appreciated. Best of all, I had the companion who flew with me in the wind during our hunts, and who was impatient to fulfill her maternal duty.

During the Queen's first pregnancy, I directed my attention to ordering the construction of my own library, and renovations to my *petits appartements,* favoring the intimacy I appreciated from my times at Château Rambouillet. In my private leisure I made my *chocolat* according to my own recipe, and sometimes even cooked some omelettes or other light meals that didn't require an oven or roaster. I'd watch the bright Apollonian egg yolk vanish into the mix, and gaze into the dark Neptunian liquid traveled all the way from the Americas to grace my lips, then inundate my mouth and veins with its earthy power, its energy merging with mine. It was my favorite reminder that France had come to own so much, and a strange—painful and pleasurable—tremor shook me to contemplate on what might happen if that should change.

Another satisfaction filled me, too, when the trial for Deschauffours sentenced him to death by burning. This sodomite deserved nothing less when he'd procured about two-hundred boys for a range of nobles and clerics, some of whom he'd kidnapped and may have even murdered. To avoid scandal there were delays to his trial, but I saw no other fitting fate for him rather than taking up space in the Bastille.

The forest called to me even in those early days of marriage, a necessary counterpart to my marriage bed. It invigorated me and I could only see the concerned glances as unfamiliarity with—and perhaps even envy of—the royal pleasure of hunting. A late July day I ignored my weak tremor and went to Rambouillet, where I fainted and had to be brought back to Versailles. Despite my growing reluctance of it, Mareschal bled me once in the arm and twice in the feet, and I wavered between recovery and feverish stupor. After more suggestions for bleeding refused by Mareschal, he took the opportunity to gently reprimand what was my undeniably growing fear. Was I close to death, yet again, as I'd been at eleven?

Mareschal recommended that I watch my boisterous entourage's feasts, and temper my ravenous appetite to avoid upsetting my stomach and general constitution. He was so earnest in his concern for me that I promised I'd temper myself in the future.

Was I passing the Queen my sickness—and she her own to me? For soon after she fell so sick that she had to be given the last rites. Thankfully she recovered, though I had the lingering impression that her dreary melancholy fueled rather than soothed mine.

We cheered up with the pleasing news of Languet's commission of the serenata *La Senna festeggiante* by Vivaldi, in honor of my rule and our Ambassador's Public Entry into Venice, as well as the painting by Canaletto of this detailed spectacle with gilded boats and crowds at the embankment next to the Palace of the Doges.

At last, after all my piety and chaste restraint, in my seventeenth year, I finally became a father of twin girls. I was delighted, for if anyone doubted I could sire children they now saw that I could do two at once. In honor of their birth, we commissioned Vivaldi for the serenata *L'unione della pace e di marte*, in fitting symbol of the union of Peace and Mars embodied by Elisabeth and Henriette.

My hunger unsatiated, I charged into the hunt with a renewed fire: if there could be two girls, there could be two boys—I chuckled secretly; thirsting, yearning for something that was so close yet still out of reach. Citing my health, Mareschal kept an ever close watch over me. In his usual caring way, I even suspected that he'd forced a bleeding that late October day—and which he knew I increasingly disliked—in order to impose me to rest, after I'd fallen out of bed from a violent nightmare and lightly scraped my knee. Though it'd been a year since I'd promised him restraint, perhaps we both knew that it might be more easily wished than accomplished.

Our third daughter Marie Louise came the following year, a striking disappointment. I was nearly uncontrollably wracked by frustration and anger at still lacking my heir the Dauphin. The lavish celebrations due for a French Dauphin were cancelled, and she instead had a mass sung for her at the chapel of Versailles in her honor.

Who could understand my gnawing restlessness? None could fathom my suffering! In fact, they seemed to want to aggravate it with the clandestine Jansenist publication, *Nouvelles ecclésiastiques,* to contest the Bull *Unigenitus,* and mock me in the process. Created at the request of Louis XIV shortly before his death, the papal bull condemned the heretical doctrines of Jansenism. I was all too glad to leave this draining matter of thick-headed men obsessed with doctrines in the hands of Cardinal Fleury, who'd surely set them in place. Even without the religious differences, I was alone as king, so there had to be a reason for my intermittent indifference to suffering.

This weight—all these generations of turmoil sitting on my shoulders—and at any moment my life could end without having an heir. As if the scar on my chest wasn't enough, though at least it could be concealed, scars appeared on my face, and the fears—always creeping at every corner—barely quieted when it was revealed to be beningn smallpox. They sang my virtuous praises in a *Poème héroïque* in their love for me, but it made little difference.

I dared not ask what Mareschal thought of me, with my years of wildness and excess. What an ignorant boy I'd been in my 'dis-ease' that was my first sign of manhood... Or when miscalculating my playful night-jump off the bed, a valet threw himself down to catch my fall, at which point I rolled under the bed, immobile. Villeroy, Poirier, and Mareschal panicked and rushed over, when my joyously sinister laugh broke my pretense of death to frighten them, and I came out of hiding on four legs. Though I was unharmed, Mareschal thoroughly checked me, found no wounds, rubbed me with some *esprit-de-vin,* allowing me to sleep soundly again under his care.

I knew he adored me, but would that be until the end? And what then? Had it all come back to haunt me, in an endless cycle of teasing and taunting that it was over—only to start all over again? Would the scars grow and get worse? In my self-hating desperation I tried to amuse myself in thinking perhaps a new mask was being made out of my face, if not my whole body.

Finally, after three daughters, on September 4th 1729, came my heir Louis, Dauphin de France. I'd been at my feverish Queen's side since her pains began and I shook with fright and delight to announce her the long-awaited news. How could I explain my whirlwind of joy? The Versailles chapel rang out with *Te Deum*, echoing my unspeakable happiness. From Paris to the provinces, prayers echoed in long succession, full of processions, fireworks and light shows, and generous gifts of coins, wine, and *petits pains*. I gifted my Queen a magnificent set for chocolate and coffee-making with dolphin motifs, merging this blessed occasion with our beloved ritual.

Three days later I was cheered as a hero when I arrived to Paris with my royal retinue of bodyguards, gendarmes, musketeers, and master falconers. I basked in the *Te Deum* at Notre Dame, watched the fireworks at l'Hôtel de Ville, and crossed the streets adorned with dazzling paper lanterns and light fixtures. That *maman* Ventadour would be appointed his Royal Governess, as she'd so loyally been to me and his sisters, was an added balm to my yearning soul.

In the midst of our insulated joy came alarming news. The Natchez had revolted against our subjects in Louisiana, massacring over two hundred of our Frenchmen and soldiers, and taking Frenchwomen, children, and slaves as captives. My blood froze as a storm raged in my soul. There'd been years of establishing our alliances with the Natchez, Choctaw, Tiou, Yazoo, and other nearby tribes. The destruction of some of our most productive Louisiana farms, and the threatened shipments of food and trade goods on the Mississippi River made the damage seem irreparable.

The account played in my mind like a horrifying tragedy. The Natchez had split up and gone into Fort Rosalie and surrounding areas where French resided. Citing their plan for a great hunt, they traded for guns, powder, and ball, and offered to pay the French even more than the usual fare. Having no reason to doubt their loyalty, the French took their poultry and corn for arms, which the Natchez then used simultaneously for their strategic revenge that sent fear flying like wild arrows across the land. A mix of disgust and intrigue consumed me. Would I do the same, were I threatened to leave my land and high temple that housed the sacred bones of my royal ancestors?

I shuddered to consider what had sparked the revolt. Had the Natchez acted alone, or had all the Indians come together in a plot to remove us? I hated the prospect of an even worse case: that the English had been behind this revolt to destroy one of our new tobacco plantations. The more time passed, the more it became clear that Perier, our Commandant-General, and his Commander de Chépart had been the abusing instigators in this unfortunate affair. I thought of our friends who'd visited but four years earlier, and hoped they were well and that their enduring loyalty would prove fruitful for us all.

Thankfully, we welcomed a second son, a year after his brother. I tried to take our little Philippe, Duc d'Anjou—whose title I'd held before taking the crown—as an omen of our continued security, and was eager to repeat the joyous celebrations of the first. But Cardinal Fleury, economical as always, deemed it unnecessary in light of our healthy Dauphin.

I was twenty years old and the father of two boys and three girls, and though eager as an Indian to keep growing our noble numbers, Cardinal Fleury thought it wise to give our frenetic duty a rest. I could gladly spend it visiting my many estates and hunting, while the Queen indulged in her music and painting passions. To add to my own art collection, Oudry—also appreciated by the Queen—astounded us with the majestically large painting of me and my entourage stag hunting in the forest of Saint-Germain. Likewise, Rigaud once more painted me in my royal regalia, this time standing and facing the other way with the hint of a smiling-serious gaze, as one hand holds the scepter and the other rests on the crown. If there were to be cycles in life then perhaps I had to vary my habits, which could offer a change from the boring routine, at least.

By then, Vivaldi's "Four Seasons" had graced the *Concert Spirituel* on several occasions and gained such popularity that I, too, fell under its spell. It seemed the most fitting tune for my life, especially the first "Spring" concerto that I often requested to be played at Marly. How joyful! How sublime a melody that banishes all anxieties! With his talent my soul turns the opening Allegro movement's heavenly violin strings to blossoming lavender and bergamot flowers, sprouting trees, bursting fountains, and birds soaring in the sky; the perpetual cycle releasing its gift of new life. In those moments I could dare to believe that the anguish that the Devil consistently tried to impose on me would not conquer and was only temporary, and that blissful happiness was not only real, but could be permanent.

But how long could the rapture last? It is just one of four seasons, and why does it so often feel like it is the briefest of all? The second melancholic Largo movement makes me think of a spring storm as if taken from the most helpless part of my soul. The blessed Venetian red-haired priest gave a tolerable face to my frightful languishing sadness and hopelessness—and I knew from that moment its miracle because I didn't shrink back from it! Engulfed in the alluring symphony I could face its dreariness and know it wouldn't last. To confirm it, the final Allegro brings renewed, gentle cheering encouragement, its passionate high and lows whispering to me of the enduring force of life-giving love from our mighty God. Sometimes a pang of jealousy filled me that the Queen might regularly experience this with music without me, even as I tried to be grateful that I experienced it at least once.

The heavenly music made by this priest seemed all the more necessary when a shocking story, soon followed by a trial in Aix-en-Provence, rattled us all. At first I was fascinated by the young woman Catherine Cadière, whose piety it was said led her to have holy convulsions, visions, and even the saintly stigmata. It then shifted to disgust and anger at her accusation that her spiritual director, a Catholic Jesuit father named Girard, had bewitched and seduced her. Were the days of the Aix-en-Provence and Loudon possessions not behind us? I had the repulsive impression of being a bewildered stag in its last living moments. What was our world coming to! How could a Jesuit dedicated to God do such a thing? Or, just as insanely, how could she not fear God and fabricate such a lie?

Naturally, the Jansenist Parlement at Aix had to gather evidence, and soon Catherine had support from parliamentarians, noble-women, and the public in Aix and Toulon. Curiously, the trial seemed to mirror my own confusion, when she was condemned to death, followed by a split verdict, until finally declared innocent. How could there be such variance? Unless... they had both been guilty and complicit? I wanted justice done and yet I sensed I would not have done much different than to forgive and release the conflicted woman, even as I wavered on what to do with the man—if guilt I could even undoubtedly establish. Death seemed too harsh—even for a Jesuit with heretical Quietist traits—while banishment could allow him to continue elsewhere. Though a relief that it was in the hands of the Parlement, I dreaded how this case might tarnish the sound Jesuits' reputation, now suspected of widespread corruption.

Yet another strange, but thankfully to me more pleasing tale appeared in the form of the wild girl of Champagne. Of all places—in France! She was first seen, dirty and cloaked in animal skins, in an orchard stealing apples from a tree at nightfall. The villagers set a dog upon her that she killed with one blow from her short club, then climbed up the tree and vanished back into the forest. Monsieur d'Epinay had her captured and confined to his estate, where she shocked them all with her sharp cries, skinning and devouring of raw rabbit and chicken, and the several washings it took to reveal her white skin. To temper her tendency to escape, Monsieur d'Epinay, with the help of the Bishop of Châlons and Governor of Champagne, had her placed at the Hôpital Général de Châlons. To begin her new life, she was baptized and named Marie-Angélique Memmie LeBlanc.

Sleep left me as I obsessed over the matter. My mind raced with the medieval tale of Valentin and Sansnom, echoed in Rabelais and others' stories, of twin brothers separated at birth; one raised as a knight in a king's court, and the other a wild man in a bear's den. Had she survived by living with the animals, maybe even fed by a she-wolf like Romulus and Remus?

I wanted to know everything about this unusual Eve: who she was, where she'd come from, and how she'd come to be in my kingdom. But even once she'd learned our language and been tamed to our ways, would she know—and share—the truth? A strange jealousy filled me to think that she surely had more in common with the Indians than with us. Worst of all was if she didn't want to stay, as her numerous escapes suggested. That she might already know of our civilized ways and had freely chosen to remove herself from them first angered, then saddened me in ways I couldn't explain.

I tormented myself at the urgent need to speak to her alone... filling me with a mix of dread and exultation. She could pounce on me and tear off my skin, or club me to death, as she'd done the dog—or as some said, another wild girl she'd argued with and wounded, maybe even killed. And I felt a delight unlike any other before to find that part of me relished the thought.

It is no apology when I say my bouts of mood swings seemed to pull me so deep that at times I had the impression of a growing—and dare I say enduring—hate for mankind. To be forced and controlled into an unwanted life... Was that how she felt? Because if so, I, as vile as it was for the King of France, to think, could share the feeling. I wallowed in that repulsive-attractive notion that in certain moments my only satisfaction was in despising them all.

I wondered if she already knew the intimate act—and with whom. Man? Woman? Both? It was said that some savages had little inhibitions about such things. Before I could rage at the thought of her being forced into the act, I smirked at the image of her fiery wild strength that promised harm to any so inclined.

Yet another daughter came, the fourth, named Adélaïde after my mother. I wondered what it was about me that seemed to bring me so many girls, until I remembered that the Queen played her part in it, too. Her increased nagging about her constant state of pregnancy did her no favors when it was entirely her purpose. Still, I did my best to ignore her nearly insulting and humiliating complaints, citing her period or my drunken breath, among other excuses, to avoid her duty. If I'd done wrong by marrying the unassuming Polish princess, at least we had two sons to carry on our Bourbon line, and we seemed set to keep delivering royal children nearly each year.

I had been more than a saint; the whole court—if not all of France—knew it. In eight years of marriage, despite all the temptations and offerings, I'd never taken a mistress, much to many others' disappointment. So while beloved by France, as a pious queen should be, I should be forgiven that I began to grow increasingly bored of my submissive, fearful wife. She'd never been able to speak to me as an equal, and though that could be endearing, especially at the shy beginning, I think part of me had hoped that would change with time. It had not, and it was becoming easier for me to consider giving another some attention. Weren't man and wife meant to share life's burdens together, as limited as the woman's role could be?

Instead of rejuvenating me with her pious devotion, the glow of her complexion had gone, and her moods and melancholy drained me, while adding to my own. Her sweet tooth had led her to bring her father Stanislas's pastry chef Nicolas with her to court, and I knew she thought of him often as she savored the mountains of dry brioche soaked in Malaga wine, and the Madeleine pastries of her father's creation. Did she wait until I was gone to recreate a past scene; where, like her father, she might enjoy them while reading *The Thousand and One Nights*, whose Ali Baba was his favorite character? The more I thought about it, I wasn't sure what I felt about his portrait hanging across her bed in her room, ever-watchful of us and anything that happened in my absence.

If all my earth-shattering, questionable ingredients had always been there, they seemed to have conspired to come together at this time. A winter cold epidemic swept through Versailles and our third daughter,

Marie Louise, was the cruel casualty. The prettiest of our daughters; my well-deserved punishment for my disappointment at her female birth, with only a mass given in lieu of celebrations only four years earlier. That she'd been baptized but a few weeks before her death was little consolation.

I secretly defied the rule that forbid mourning a Daughter of France if under the age of seven by letting the devastation fester inside me. Why should I share others' pain when I couldn't express mine unless under strict specific cases! At times I swore, and was almost even sure, that it might explode someday, and I wallowed in that sense of pathetic revenge, too. Though I could hardly look at her portrait by Gobert in her blue dress, I tried to imagine her flying free with the two bird companions painted at her side.

I'd known sadness all my life, but there is none like losing a child, and in my self-hate I knew that even that horrible revelation was a form of undeserved grace. I was a monster, but I took solace in realizing that I could also mourn my child in a shattering way I'd never imagined. Some days I thought my grief would consume me, and though I wanted to share in my pregnant Queen's suffering, I often had to keep my distance and keep wearing Versailles' required mask of composure.

I was twenty-three, had wealth and a growing family, yet I still felt alone. I needed support, and as dark times may reveal true friends, I found that I had it in someone other than my consort. It was not a beauty who first caught my attention, but one whose discretion, natural good mood devoid of ambition, and playful care for her appearance gradually brought us together.

Louise Julie de Mailly-Nesle was my age and also married, and though Cardinal Fleury favored her, I took no pleasure in knowing it was a double adultery and mortal sin. But I was also a man; could God not forgive me for seeking natural comfort when my Queen couldn't provide it? Louise Julie was from an ancient noble family from the northern region of Picardy, and her mother—the spirited Armande Félice who'd fought a duel over a lover—had been a lady-in-waiting to the Queen until passing the office to her daughter at her death. Thankfully, Louise Julie seemed as docile and discreet as her philandering parents had been known for their scandalous affairs in the time of the Regent.

Should I have stopped then? Or was it just another reminder that nothing would ever truly be in my hands? For God saw fit to chastise me yet again by striking us with the death of our second son, the Duc d'Anjou. He'd always been a sickly child in Mareschal's caring hands, but his frail two-year old body yielded to the seizure that gripped him. My anguish was more than I could ever describe, when he'd died without having been baptized. I knew myself unworthy to pray, but I forced myself, begging God to accept him despite my sin. As my gutwrenching tears flowed, I tried to wrap his and his sister's memory in the faint echo of Vivaldi's "Spring" resonating in my thoughts, wanting them to forever remain in such an angelic embrace. Something broke in me and I knew that I would never be the same or forgive myself. I kept distance from Louise Julie, resolving to abandon our sinful relations, yet doubting my own strength and resolve at every moment.

Our fifth daughter came the next month, named Victoire, after myself and our ancestor, the wife of Louis XIV. Blurry, inebriated months passed in trying to adjust to two missing children, the hunts offering me a bloody-black escape. How I'd wanted to bring them along someday, but it was not meant to be. But why shouldn't I have, even as babies!—I raged. What were these courtly laws; what pathetic, emotionless vile king had to hesitate before showing too much affection to his children, or doing something considered out of etiquette! Surely the Indians hadn't fashioned for themselves such cruel restrictions! A putrid suffocating cloud hung over me intermittently and I tried to see them more often, wanting to wallow with them as their *Papa-roi* in their childish innocence that filled the Princes' Wing, so rare in a court full of impurity, greed, and intrigue.

Another war erupted, when the Polish King Augustus II died and set off the War of Polish Succession. Naturally we supported the

Queen's father Stanislas as the nation's rightful successor, and with my uncle King Philip V of Spain as our ally, we were faced against Austria, Russia, and Prussia who supported Augustus's son as heir. A series of campaigns launched across the continent, whose winter halt seemed little helpful in containing the Habsburg expanding power and securing Stanislas's crown.

I had some consolation in my secret relations with Louise Julie, whose desire for nothing other than myself only increased my wish to cover her in gifts, had I the means—unchecked by Cardinal Fleury—to do it. I relished the days at La Muette, Rambouillet, or at Mademoiselle de Charolais's Château de Madrid where I'd see Louise Julie, and feel something like the allure of being—or dare I say becoming—momentarily another person. I don't know which is more proper to say: that I wished I was feeling this way because of her, or because of something else, calling to me, begging for me to try and wear as many masks as possible, as befitting a king. The idea by turns terrified and seduced me.

We had a sixth daughter, Sophie, and at Christmas I was still too wracked by my torment of guilt and impurity to partake in the holy duty of offering my royal touch to those suffering of scrofula. Who was I to cure this King's Evil when I had lost two children and taken on a secret mistress? I dared not say it, but what if I was to pass on my sins to someone else in the process—or theirs to me—when sin so often seems easier to catch than goodness? Yet I was fascinated, too, at the way the sickly trusted in this power they were so sure—or at least hoped—I had when I myself doubted it most. Was it worse for me to refuse, despite my sin, when it might be a humbling chance for me to witness His grace once more? Yet the Devil fixed on me, when in March the Queen delivered a stillborn son. Three children dead, two of them sons. And yet the king had to go on, wearing his main mask of unshakeable strength and endurance.

My mind drifted in its familiar dark mazes of mangled bodies, odd shapes and sounds, reeking of blood-iron and gun-powder, and bitter wine aftertaste. I'd always needed distraction, but a longing to escape intensified. I pondered Parisians' disappointment at Rameau's new opera-ballet *Les Indes Galantes*, inspired by the Indian embassy that had graced my court ten years before. I chuckled like the fifteen-year old I'd been as I imagined they'd be as pleased with it as they'd been with what they'd seen of the opera.

More pleasantly, I relished the timely ongoing developments of my plans for the third floor above the *petits appartements*, renovated as my *Petits cabinets* to reflect my love of hunting and longing for smaller gatherings and intimacy. While some of the rooms faced out onto the château's Marble Courtyard, most clustered around interior courtyards, with my favorite of them being the *Cour des Cerfs*. The sculpted stag heads adorning its walls were as much reminders of my hunting successes as they made inspirational guiding companions. I also welcomed the new private semicircular staircase that very few others than myself would step in, and considered the kind of pieces I might adorn this space leading to my growing cabinet of curiosities.

To ensure that my private *petits soupers* following the hunts would be a deliciously informal affair, my personal cook Jean-Baptiste Lazure was granted his own *cabinets*. I mused that he might teach me some of his cooking tips just as much as I loved incorporating flying tables with compartments to limit the need for servants.

As Louis XIV had done for some of his hunting dogs, I also built a new room for my prized creatures, where I adored treating them to their daily biscuit. For much-needed quieter contemplation, in the ever-expanding library I might read about plants from Linnaeus or hunting and fishing by Boudet, while surrounded by detailed maps and enthralling scenes of stag, boar, fox, and rabbit hunting that sent my mind yearning to be out there doing the same—or, I often fanta-sized, with even more exotic prey.

Based on the Chevalier de Beringhen's hunting portrait, Oudry also painted me in my brown hunting attire embroidered with gold, wearing a self-satisfied smile, as I pet a Pointer at one side, and hold a dead partridge by its leg in the other. These quarters were to be my refuge, an extension of my need of and gratitude for hunting and privacy, where the lower ceilings and narrower spaces drew me and my small entourage closer together in the throes of its triumphant final embrace.

The Queen birthed our seventh daughter Thérèse, and in my un-relenting yearning for new, different and exotic hunting scenes for my private apartments, I finally commissioned six of the greatest artists for the task. The result was a *Leopard Hunt* by Boucher, a *Lion Hunt* by de Troy, a *Tiger Hunt* by Lancret, and a *Chinese Hunt* by Pater. But my favorites were Parrocel's *Elephant Hunt* and Van Loo's *Bear Hunt*. I wondered if Louis XIV would approve of the new art, for even he had sought some privacy at Trianon away from the court.

Perhaps it was the living art that filled me with fire, for I resumed my duty as healing king and resisted my relations with Louise Julie. Though the Queen had begun to suspect my relations with Louise Julie, who was her lady-in-waiting, I could take some comfort in the knowledge that it was not always a lie that at times I had no interest in either of them.

Shortly before Christmas that year, my dear Mareschal died, my trusted surgeon who'd so often cared for my and my family's lives leaving me alone for another world. I sobbed like a child, doubting that any would ever counsel me and watch over my health as he'd so carefully done. Hoping he'd watch over me from the beyond, I tried to console myself that at least *maman* Ventadour, since replaced by her strict granddaughter Marie Isabelle, was still alive.

Striving for the right path, I kept up my healing duty, filled with insatiable fiery energy that had to be divine. And then, another mask revealed itself to me: be free and venture out incognito! After discreetly informing the Queen with a note, I slipped on my domino and with a few confidants, we cavorted to the opera. So this was the thrill that oth-ers knew and indulged in, while the King of France had to be a prisoner of his own identity! Yet before I could begin to settle in my inebriated pleasure, I was recognized by two guards. We vanished out of there, relieved that no one—other than my most trusted valets Bachelier and Lebel—would know which woman I'd gone to see, while hating the concern that Cardinal Fleury might hear of this escapade. Enraged that the adventure had been so brief, yet not devoid of its thrills, I mused that there'd be more of them, especially during my consort's monthly flow, followed closely by my valets.

I kept it to myself that I even thought of stealing away to see Marie-Angélique, the feral wild girl who dwelled at a provincial estate in Châlons. In public, I'd say that the girl had made great progress and improvements with our language and civilized manners, evident through her cleanliness and her use of fine silverware. Yet secretly I'd wish nothing less than to see her savagely eating raw animal flesh, the blood and juices saturating and trickling down her hands and arms to the tune of her eager chewing... To think that she'd learned to tame the first impulse pleased me, and I wanted to tell her that if she'd felt alone, she could make others—even me—feel less so, too. While I imagined that she'd like that Linnaeus' *Systema naturae* aimed to remove legend and superstition from science by explaining the species of monsters—of which some would say she was a part—I might've liked it more that she might not care at all.

Soon after we had the visit of the most illustrious Venetian eunuch opera singer Farinelli, invited by the Queen to give her music lessons. I couldn't help but notice his melancholic dark eyes and pursed lips, and observe his long form and massive thighs to match his unmutated voice they called *voce bianca*.

To the sound of his celebrated unearthly vocals, my mind soared, wanting to ask him so many things. Had his castration been worth having a voice that was neither male nor female? Was this what he'd always wanted, and how did he feel; to be seen with wonder and admiration? Did his art make him forget everything, maybe even the secret insults and disgust of being a misshapen man-made monster?

Likewise I wavered in settling on him not having any desires of the flesh, or that he'd already experienced at least some of them. Though I believed in the occasional soothing powers of music, his talent did not—and I believe nothing would—surpass his fellow Venetian Vivaldi's heavenly "Spring" segment of "Four Seasons." I gifted him a golden snuffbox and my portrait set in diamonds and he went on to the Spanish court.

Concurrent with Farinelli's departure was the birth of our eighth daughter, Louise. Though I'd only mind her small head and frame insofar as it threatened her life, I did not comment on it, even as I sensed an even deeper distance from the Queen, a cold desperation from my consort that had become as familiar as repulsive. There was little either of us could do if God chose to give us daughters instead of sons. After some coaxing she confessed that her doctors feared for her life should she have further pregnancies, but that she would gladly suffer to give me another Duc d'Anjou. Well and good, when many were honored to die in the act of giving life! But what did these doctors know? And what would I do? How I wished Mareschal was there to counsel me and tell me the truth!

Was it also partly her childish way of voicing her wish to end her charge of bearing royal children? Yet even in her piety I refused to believe that she would want me in another's arms. She would keep doing her duty, which despite all the daughters, had proven fruitful so far. I liked to think that was as much my husbandly right as her sincere wish to keep pleasing me. When asked what to name our new daughter until her baptism, I defiantly said Madame the Last, as much from growing likelihood as wishful thinking for sons.

To distract myself I had my lathe and comfortable accompanying chair moved to the fourth floor of my private apartments, grateful for this humble turning hobby even as some teased me for it, as they did my demeaning wish to cook some simple stews. All the same, prized were my wood or ivory snuffboxes as New Year's gifts.

Another late night I ventured out around Versailles, once again disguised with my entourage. We ran into two women we didn't know, and to disarm them, Mademoiselle de Charolais approached them to discover the troubling matter. Before I knew it, I couldn't resist stepping forth, incognito, assuring the charming hotelkeeper as I pressed her close to me that I could be of assistance. Amidst her confusion, the captain of the guards Villeroy then tried to seduce her, as my cousin burst into laughter. Aggravated, the woman angrily shook out of my grasp, citing her honorable status and complaining at the king and his guards' incapacity of ensuring women's safety, even at the very gates of the château.

To my shock, what had started as mere amusement had turned into embarrassment, and I realized then that a part of me had been aware that such gossip of our outings—if it came to that—might spread, but that I didn't care. As La Rochefoucauld said, if there are men whose ridiculousness has never been found, it's that we didn't search well enough. Could a king not have some fun in his own kingdom? No one was harmed, and even if I should earn some pamphlets for it, in a sense it'd been my own making; perhaps even my own self-punishment. For once, I even hoped that my subjects might see in it some unexpected humor, and that if the English monarch could suffer some of it from his own, I should be able to do the same.

As the court considered the question of my mistress, Cardinal Fleury set his displeased eyes on my youngest daughters, whose high-ranking titles entitled them to costly demands. Concerned, he advised our five youngest Mesdames to be sent to the prestigious Abbey of Fontevraud, based under the rule of Saint Benedict and resting place of the Plantagenets monarchs. Cardinal Fleury had taken into account my consideration to announce my official mistress, whose costs he minded less, so long as she—and any others—stayed out of his affairs. Though I wanted my children near, I did not protest, swallowing back my shattering emotion behind the increasingly heavy Versailles mask that I daily half hoped would suffocate me out of my misery. I consoled myself by thinking that time would pass quickly until they'd return at their adult age of fifteen.

Words will fail me in fully articulating how annoyed and nervous I was when the Day of Exposure came. It was a warm July day, when at my beloved Compiègne I announced that I would sup at Louise Julie's, thus officially announcing my favorite. In a sense, I wanted to congratulate myself. It was no small feat to have kept our relation, no matter how platonic in its first few years, entirely secret for eight years! But to relinquish it was a triumph of sorts, and even my permission to create yet other secrets. If nothing else, this should lay to rest the questions of who to set for the task of being my mistress. Judging by the way some portrayed it, I would've liked to feel as the presumed "free, libertine man" of my times, but almost as soon as I said it, it already had formed its own air of duty and formality that I knew I'd never fully escape.

On my return from Compiègne, I visited the Queen for our conjugal duty. She refused to open the door. When I tried again, I spent four hours in her bed trying to convince her of our duty, to which she wouldn't listen, citing the doctor's orders to refuse all maternity. What had happened to wanting it at all costs, even that of her life for the chance of giving us another son? Ashamed at my rejection, I decided then that it was the last time I'd ever ask it of her.

In the solitude of my tearful despair I tried to make sense of it. What had I done wrong? I did not lack physical beauty, when I was described as such and girls and women longed for my attention. D'Argenson had even said I looked like Love at my coronation! Was *maman*, the gentle Madame de Ventadour, the only woman I could ever trust? How could my consort, ordained by God, do this to me? I, who'd raised her from her humble Polish roots to become the Queen to the greatest kingdom in Europe—even on earth! I, who'd put up with her superstitious fears of nightly spirits! Despite my presence, she'd request her chambermaid stay the night to hold her hand and recite her tales until she fell asleep, at which point I quietly retreated to my own bed for much-needed sleep! I who'd been so nervous at her first pregnancy, limiting my hunts and canceling my Fontainebleau visits! All of Paris had rejoiced, the Bastille's canons had blasted off in celebration as we'd given them two children at once. Could it really be over? My entourage had once amused themselves in citing a list of beautiful women, while I'd found my Queen even more beautiful than them—it'd been true for me no matter the obvious or concealed sneers.

Who had turned her against me? Was it Cardinal Fleury with his sermons, concerned of her taking me away from him? I knew he did not care for her, and he had his reasons. Though my consort had angered me in a way I'd never imagined, no one would ever take her place nor could she, or did I want her to be replaced. To my torment were added the whispers against Louise Marie's supposed inferiority for not being beautiful enough to be my mistress, fueling her insecurity.

In my struggle for self-control, I resorted to myself for a time to release my own consuming chaos. But it was not the same. How could it be? If self-pleasure was sufficient, would anyone have relations with others? To this day I am both proud and ashamed that I still had some naïve wish that I might still manage—and even conquer—in that self-reliant way. I violently tossed and turned at night, sweaty, crying, groaning, until I got up and seized a cold blade and pressed it against my groin—panting and swearing I'd become an emasculated *musico* like her Farinelli, and then everyone would blame her for what she did to me! I doubled over in pain like an outcast orphan, hating her even as I loved the cruel mourning of all that we'd created.

Gradually a kind of grace visited me, and I realized that I was harming myself with endless questions and guilt. The Great Chain of Being, with my place near the top. Did I really have to worry? To think that I, the divinely chosen king of the powerful French kingdom should be rejected by his wife, and then pine for her, was practically laughable! What's more, the Queen was praying enough for the both of us, if not for the whole kingdom! If she wanted it that way, then so it would be, and she would have no more of my attention beyond the customary requirements. I would show my deepest feelings even less, with her and with everyone else. Satisfaction filled me at the thought that in some Eastern cultures it was forbidden to gaze upon the monarch's face. Who could dare to think they knew me! No one would have the privilege of knowing my true self!

After all these years of doing my duty and rejecting the suggestions to take a mistress, it seemed my time had come to embrace it and let myself be served. I, the king, had rejected what other men had at leisure—and thus a new door opened. If the heroic, chivalrous love of Louis XIV's time had now been replaced with licentiousness, perhaps it was time I had a shameless, freeing taste of it, too. Perhaps it might even have the effect of taming my need, and there was my initially reluctant yet alluring opportunity to find out.

As such, our separate lives went on. The Queen had her amusements in her favorite *cavagnole* game of chance—whose great debts I was increasingly reluctant to pay—and painting and music hobbies, her most popular being her weekly Polish choral concerts. I had my hunting, woodturning hobby, books, and new glorious hunting paintings. Unlike the portrait he'd painted of Mariana Victoria of Spain and I years before, I had de Troy's *Hunting Meal* scene made with its companion, the *Death of a Stag*, and hung in my dining room at Fontainebleau. Likewise I added Van Loo's *The Hunting Halt* to the collection, another tableau with well-dressed courtiers lunching in a bucolic landscape. I welcomed the main couple in the foreground who flirted while eating, and that it could easily be assumed to be myself with a mistress, or anyone other than my consort.

As I stared and followed the other hunters in the background, the scene might morph, as ferocious beasts emerged unexpectedly to stampede into the picnic, and devour the hunters in revenge, or simply delayed famished hunger. I'd watch them all perish—a fitting punishment for at least some of them—as I was left to roam alone, or even invited to join the beasts and be their king in the heart of nature where no one would ever find me.

I'd spend hours lost in the contemplation that while I'd never dare to order a painting of such a gruesome scene, I took comfort in knowing it dwelled somewhere in the recesses of my mind, as if protecting me with its vengeful might.

Surely it was only my imagination... but why see such things? What a horrible person I had to be to have such vile ideas! Or—no; it was a higher, stronger power talking to me, showing me its chaos and I was just witnessing it! I tried not to look, but it was too strong, and to my horror I realized it was trying to *seduce* me into its world. Would I go? No... But would I always be able to resist it? I repeated to myself a prayerful plea that if I froze it would leave my pitiful unsure form and sneer as it left me shaken up, as it awaited another moment.

For the gardens of Versailles I ordered the completion of the Neptune Basin, pleased to add my mark to Louis XIV's legacy. And as a counter to our more beastly inclinations, I amused myself to think that he'd also favor my addition of personal water closets with running water to my private apartments. While I saw the benefit of having them everywhere in the château, it was also fitting for some to have to either wallow in their own excrement, or to worry about its disposal, should they even care about sanitation.

Since new acquisitions were in order, I added three other unofficial beneficiary women to my royal trysts, all the while Louise Julie remained my official mistress. What were a few more, when I was honoring them with my kingly desires? Quick and dismissive was all I needed. I also met Louise Julie's younger, loud and witty sister Pauline Félicité, whom she introduced to the court and whose lingering teasing gaze on me allured me.

News spread of King Charles VII's villa being built at Portici, and the continuing excavations at Herculaneum, near Pompeii, begun by his predecessor. I longed to be there, to inhale the deadly volcanic ash left by Mount Vesuvius's eruption in October 79 AD, as I dug into its ancient secrets and treasures. The thought of the countless young women who'd suffocated as they were buried alive made me both want to preserve and release them. I resolved that it would only be a matter of time until French specialists would lend their knowledge to the affair.

At this time it was decided that my nearly twelve-year-old firstborn, my beloved Elisabeth, would marry her nineteen-year-old cousin, Infante Philip of Spain. I wanted this affair to supersede the failed engagement of my younger years with Mariana Victoria—who was Philip's older sister, and who, like my Queen, seemed to give her husband only daughters—and show the world the power of the French monarchy. Signing the Treaty of Vienna, finally officially ending the War of Polish Succession, reminded me all the more why I wanted it so.

Austria and Russia had succeeded in supporting their Polish candidate Augustus III, requiring the Queen's father Stanislas to renounce his claim to the Polish throne and to recognize Augustus. In exchange, he was compensated with the duchies of Lorraine and Bar, which would revert back to France upon his death. I wavered between a lingering sense of defeat and acceptance in light of my ambivalence on helping him acquire a crown. If his daughter was any indication, what loyalty could I expect from him? As I was learning, not even a King of France could always get what he wanted.

It remained that I was to give away one of my children in marriage for the first time, and therefore worthy celebration had to be in order. The Hercules Room was inaugurated with a grand ball to announce the news, featuring the Biblical paintings *Rebecca at the Well* and *Feast in the House of Simon* by Veronese facing each other on the walls. But all eyes were on the new majestic ceiling by François Lemoyne, showing *The Apotheosis of Hercules* raised to the rank of the gods after his labors.

When the affair finally shifted to an evening masked ball, I whirled around in my bat mask, inquiring as to the king's whereabouts... And basked in Lemoyne's glorious achievement adorning this former chapel site, grateful that at least it hadn't been the last thing he worked on before stabbing himself nine times in the throat and chest with his smallsword... If only rewarding him with the highest title of *First painter to the King* had been enough...

Eager to shake off the familiar sense of loss, I did not fail to return to a certain person increasingly worthy of my attention.

The boldness—or was it self-hating destruction?—seemed to overcome me again, when I flatly refused the scrofula ceremony in Easter. But in my conflicted vanity I prayed that it was better to display some form of honesty—no matter how repulsive—than to keep up that charade. That I was an adulterer seemed a fitting reason not to confess, take communion, or partake in the scrofula ritual ceremony; though Cardinal Fleury did all he could to encourage me to confess and renounce my mistress, to no avail.

Did I not care what the believing French public thought? How could I reject the sacred ceremonies so dear to them, and to the enduring ancient French monarchy itself! The tempest thundered over me constantly. And why, as king, should I have given it more thought than I already did? I cared about my kingdom's affairs, I took advice and avoided conflict, and I was not the first king to have a mistress. Cardinal Fleury had his affairs to handle, and I had mine.

I feigned a reconciliation with the Queen, all the better to dissimulate my bond with Louise Julie, and added Desportes' painting of my hunting dogs Pompée and Florissant to my collection. And yet, amidst everything, Pauline Félicité fiery mischievous personality lingered in my thoughts ever since the ball, and I shook with delicious pleasure at the lingering prospect of making her mine, too, in due time.

Having managed to prolong my daughter's stay with us by my insistence on the wedding only happening once she turned twelve, Elisabeth's marriage contract was signed by proxy in late summer. Though her royal dowry exceedingly alarmed Cardinal Fleury, the lavish celebrations stretched for days all the way to Paris, with fireworks, a nautical parade on the Seine, and a masked ball with thousands of prominent nobles in attendance.

Heavy was my heart on the day of Elisabeth's departure—the fiery half to her gentle twin Henriette—and I couldn't help but get into her carriage to accompany her up to Plessis-Piquet. It had been hardest for Henriette, and at least I could selfishly console myself that she was who was so calm, intelligent, and peaceful was staying with me, along with the ten-year-old Dauphin, and seven-year-old Adélaïde.

My hunting had competition in turning my attention to Pauline Félicité. There was no use denying it: I had fallen under her spell, and I took the steps to make her my second mistress. I assured Louise Julie that she would remain my official mistress, and that I loved Pauline Félicité as much as I did her. I was touched by her ultimately yielding, tearful resolve to my confession, and I wished that she could see that, at least in a way, it wasn't entirely untrue. To become my mistress Pauline Félicité had to be married, and in doing so, she became de Marquise de Vintimille.

If it seemed strange, or even sacrilegious to love two sisters, I hardly thought of them as such, when they were so different while having the benefit of belonging to the same illustrious ancient royal family. As if I could plan how I felt about someone! Pauline's unapologetic cheerfulness pierced my heart and I couldn't—and wouldn't—resist.

Ambitious and confident in my royal abilities, she drew out the grand monarch in me that was often too glad to yield to Cardinal Fleury. Around her another, better version of myself emerged, beckoning and fueling a confidence that yearned to be more firmly and permanently established.

Not least of all were our delicious nights, when I relished tasting her tender breasts and long neck, and being wrapped in her taller form imbued in her signature animal scent that announced its undeniable musky presence. Shedding our masks, our presumed proud, distant natures dissolved into a mutual understanding of our dislike for our world of manipulation. In our pleasurable throes, I thought that for the first time I had found my match in every way, and the one who'd understand unpleasant things about myself I'd never dreamed of sharing.

In a sense, it even delighted me that the court might find plenty to revile and secretly insult, when it was increasingly a kind of triumph to go against, or at least dismiss their short-sighted, jealous opinions. If some hated her for her so-called arrogance, she was certainly better than at least some of them. Best of all, my happiness was such that I not only didn't care, but often hoped they'd rot in their perpetual petty envy.

Did nature have a will of its own, ready to attack at any moment? Could poison ever be a good, or useful, thing? I dreaded it myself, gorging on fruits and meat after my hunting trips, though any man needed the best food he could get. Mushrooms seemed harmless enough, except when Emperor Charles VI poisoned himself with them the night of a hunt. Though the Habsburgs had been our long-time enemy—and one with whom we'd just exchanged territories in the Polish Succession War—I wished such a fate on no one. I tried to take it as an inadvertent warning to myself, while pondering that it could be our opportunity to challenge Habsburg power, with Spain and Prussia's support. The twenty-three year old Maria Theresa—another mother of daughters—stood as the rightful heir, but how reliable would be an inexperienced woman's rule, if she inherited the crown? Or, as per tradition, it might go to her husband instead. Impressively, they could at least count on the support of Hanover, the Dutch Republic, and Britain.

The news filled the court with longing for glory, in part left unfulfilled by the Polish Succession War. It spread like wildfire, with all manners of men going so far as to accuse the pacifist Cardinal Fleury of cowardice. No matter the course, it seemed inevitable that we would all get pulled into this theatre from which everyone wanted a satisfying reward.

I celebrated the new year by gifting Pauline Félicité a gold inlaid snuffbox, which was as suggestive of our relation as it was common to give gifts for the occasion.

It was at this time that my younger cousin Louis-François, the Prince de Conti started coming to my attention. With his discreet, reserved nature, acute mind and military daring—perhaps in part inherited from the Grand Condé as but one of his illustrious ancestors who'd participated in the Frondes—I turned to him for trusted council.

He even proposed to marry Henriette, and though I sympathized with him having recently lost a stillborn son and his wife in childbirth, I refused as much for his insufficient rank as for his notorious libertine ways. Henriette at least partially agreed, when she claimed to be in love with her cousin, Louis Philippe d'Orléans, Duc de Chartres. It was yet another match I had to refuse, to prevent our power falling into the House of Orléans. I did not enjoy whatever youthful pain my daughter suffered at this, but a part of me preferred she remained unmarried and free to pursue her music passion than make a less than ideal match. With the ongoing Austrian affairs shaking up the whole continent, the best place for my cousin seemed to be at the front, where I hoped he'd soon forget any lingering disappointment over that prospect.

Fittingly, my children were attached to their mother and one another, with the eleven-year-old Dauphin leading his sisters like the firm yet good prince he already seemed intent on being. I'd been momentarily concerned when in his younger years he'd been difficult and uncooperative with his education. But gradually, his rigorous schedule of languages, ancient Greek and Latin, history, geography, astronomy, philosophy, along with music and drawing managed to capture his attention.

As for whatever blame could be laid upon me for my transgressions, I did my best to continue to be discreet. Though my absence could be ascribed more to my hunting enthusiasm than anything else, the Queen could also amuse herself and the children with her parents' fall visits from their court in Nancy. I envied her closeness to her father Stanislas—who stayed at the Grand Trianon, where Tsar Peter the Great had stayed during his visit when I was but a tender seven-year-old—and took solace at his approval at the sight of the progress of the Neptune fountain.

With my recent acquisition of the Château de Choisy, crucially neighbored by the forest of Sénart, I prompted my chosen architect, Ange-Jacques Gabriel, to enlarge it. Once completed, I gifted it to Pauline Félicité, who was with child, and gladly spent less time at Versailles in favor of being there with her and our entourage who enjoyed a relaxed etiquette. I liked to think of it as a good sign that the former owner, Marie Anne de Bourbon, was the legitimized daughter of Louis XIV and his first mistress, Louise de la Vallière, and also his favorite daughter.

Despite my passionate love for Pauline Félicité, I kept to my duty by attending the *Conseil* meetings at Versailles on Wednesdays and Thursdays, and even gladly attended the inauguration of the finished Neptune Basin, whose hydrolic system of water jets made a striking display amidst the lead sculptures. Inspired, I also commissioned Oudry for the first painting of bizarre stag antlers from a stag I slayed. Shown in sideview, it displays a long antler with five tines resting against a wall, and the other side amputated with only the brow tine.

But I gladly rushed back to my smaller, beautiful abode for my other intimate family life and our beloved *petits soupers*. I sensed the aging and ailing Cardinal Fleury's displeasure at my absence but I enjoyed, if not needed, that distance, too.

Having already displayed my independent ruling capability during his sickness, Pauline Félicité had even suggested I work with the ministers from Choisy, but I didn't want intrusions into our sacred, and unfortunately surely temporary, more private arrangements.

At last she showed signs of giving birth, which I looked forward to in part to be rid of her horrible mood swings. But all of that meant nothing in the face of yet another life that was joining our small intimate circle. I remained at her side, feeling useless as the surgeon La Peyronie, successor to my beloved Mareschal, tended to her. To my joy, she birthed a healthy son, Charles, but her fever was such to extend my nervous worry. Days passed in tormenting fear as she feverishly agonized, convinced she'd been poisoned. But how? By whom! It couldn't be—and it wasn't just my pride in raging at the thought that someone would dare tarnish our precious haven.

The doctors decided to bleed her feet, and when her pain worsened, she called for her confessor. Racked by convulsions, she died in his arms before she could confess, leaving me heartbroken. What was a son without his mother—did I not know enough of that lonely pain? What could I possibly be to him now, without her to raise him, and my near absence required by courtly affairs? And yet, how did I dare to complain! I prayed that the mass given in her honor might kill my sinful thoughts, before I accumulated more curses on myself.

My self: I was the one responsible for her state of damnation, when her pregnancy had been painful for months, and she'd been unable to confess on time. From somewhere I thought I heard a devilish sneer, satisfied with the cruel decree: I could not have them both, when it knew I'd preferred for her to stay alive so that we could try all over again, in our intoxicating, triumphant embraces.

Refusing to see the Queen and after granting Cardinal Fleury only a few minutes, I gave orders to have her portrait done, as well as her bust, as much to commemorate her beauty as to overcome the horror of her last sufferings. I took it as another sign of her defiant strength that it took two men to hold her chin shut during the sculpture moulding.

I spent a month mourning far from court in Saint-Léger near Rambouillet, my grief little eased by the autopsy that revealed no signs of poison. She was gone all the same, and it was too soon! She'd given me a son on the first try; how many more could we have had? But all I could think was that he was the reason for his mother's disappearance, and I couldn't accept that—and wasn't sure I ever would.

There was my lingering rage too, my thirst for bloody revenge that I hoped was an eternally bonding blend of Pauline's and my wishes. How could I forgive such barbaric *lèse-majesté*? What if I chose to punish the guards who'd left her body unattended, and had them mutilated the way her body had been, in their hate for "the king's whore"? How criminally base for these vile subjects to spit their joy and insults at the procession taking her body to its final rest at the chapel Saint-Louis! What would, and should, I do—and if I was hated so much then why strive to be loved by them? I, who'd refused to profane the sacraments just to keep up appearances—another sanctioned lie—and at least tried to show myself truthfully despite my flaws! They would've never dared with any of Louis XIV's mistresses! The more I thought, the more I perceived the torrent of indignation, by turns stirred and soothed by Champagne. But it was just a temporary cage-body—I tried to convince myself—and she was beyond their savagery.

I listened to the mass, read spiritual texts, still attended the Councils at Versailles. Even the Salon's thrilled communal reception of the bizarre stag antlers I commissioned from Oudry a few months before left me indifferent. How could they, or anyone, understand? Surely it was just another *trompe-l'œil* piece to gossip about, an unusual oddity of one majestic antler with the other short and deformed, nothing more. And yet I relished that only I knew the extent of its incarnation: the cacophony of hunting horn and swarming greyhounds; the stifling heat; the urgency of cutting off the testicles and slicing into hairy flesh, spraying out its perfume of fresh, warm blood; Oudry's hands and paints mixing with the fluids in mysterious sanctified creation... I resolved that it would be the first in a series to adorn my private staircase, where very few others would ever step. Perhaps it was only too fitting, for though I suspected, and even hoped for its lingering striking effect on the public, the unfortunate timing of its presentation only further shrouded it—and me—in lonely despair.

Seeking out her essence, I'd read her letters and stare at Nattier's portrait of her as Flora, exposing her lovely breast... my tears contorting her long neck and sunken face with drooping mouth into a harrowing stag head mount. Her dark vacant eyes fixed away were worse than if she'd locked them on me. Had she forgotten me already, found a happier place elsewhere, this precious kindred soul that left me too soon? Sometimes, transfixed and still as a statue, I could hear the faint tune of Vivaldi's "Spring," and I pinched a smile as I thought I'd glimpsed her in a garden with my angelic children.

In our shared mourning, Louise Julie and I grew close again, and if her time of atonement spent washing the poor's feet wasn't enough, she also wanted to raise our son to honor us both. I agreed, at least until the boy would be baptized at Pauline's husband's estate, and raised there by his adoptive father.

I began the new year by becoming grandfather for the first time, my first-born Elisabeth having birthed a girl, Isabelle, in Madrid. Though I may not have missed her as much as did her twin Henriette, it cheered me to think of my daughter having earned her respected place at the Spanish court. Philip was a passive husband who accepted her energetic personality and wish for an independent position worthy of their birth, and her net of loyal contacts at Versailles—among them her siblings—were dedicated to her aspirations.

I remained a flawed man and monarch, but I was still divinely appointed. My debilitating mourning had a treatment, as temporary and displeasing as it was. I—who still mourned my parents and brother, my lost youth, my two children, Mareschal, my wife's rejection, and now my mistress despised by the people—could be forgiven my restlessness. I grew bored of the self-effacing Louise Julie and set my eye on her younger sister Hortense. Though she was unhappily married, Hortense refused, wishing only to enjoy her place at court, independent of her husband. I stifled my self-loathing even as I pondered that she could change her mind.

I was then struck by the youngest and prettiest of the sisters, the widow Marie Anne, attired in Chinese dress at the Dauphin's masked ball. Yet she, too, was uninterested in becoming my mistress, given her attachment to her lover. My shock at her refusal fueled my wounded desire, and when her lover was revealed to have fallen to another, she finally surrendered to me. If it was her revenge to him, it was part of mine, too, when I was beginning to wish for these sisters—except for the ever-gentle Louise Julie—to fight and compete amongst each other for my favor.

But I underestimated her games when, her cruel capriciousness surpassing her beauty, Marie Anne stated her conditions that she be made Duchess with a permanent income and court position, and that Louise Julie leave Versailles. My dear Louise Julie; the one who'd been my first, and so far longest loyal mistress, uninterested in riches and who'd opened the court to her younger sisters by her selfless, unsuspecting invitations! Even my Queen, who'd been most hurt by this first transgression, preferred Louise Julie to Marie Anne. That Marie Anne would demand to be thus courted when the others had easily accepted oscillated between an affront and a necessary challenge.

I pondered over it as I commissioned Oudry for a second bizarre stag antlers, this time with shorter, and more even velvety antlers and some exposed flesh. In my desperate yearning for privacy, I resolved that it would be the second and last time that pieces from this private art collection would grace the Salon.

And I yielded: offering a pension for Louise Julie—for herself and infant Charles—and lavished Marie Anne with her required apartments, a carriage, a pension, and a title, as I yearned to capture and subdue this haughty, demanding beauty who seemed to think herself superior to everyone, and even me.

She held out on me for so long that when I finally had this cold, calculating, plump Venus under me, I was as rough and uncaring of her feigned gracefulness as I could be. As such, I enjoyed every moment of her plaintive yet pleasured moaning bursting out of her small mouth and terrified large almond eyes. If she'd thought to spare herself the so-called humiliation of being a temporary mistress to the king with her endless demands, I could show her it was still possible to put her there in the most secret—and revealing—of ways. She was just like all the others eager to manipulate and bleed me dry, and I would get my satisfaction in turn. That first night I knew that if there was something about me that led to women's destruction, I relished the thought that she would experience its effects in due time.

To add to my pleasure, I had some new dalliance with her remaining and favorite sister Diane Adélaïde, whom, in her predictable vanity, she didn't think of as a threat. When would these parasitic petty nobles, and everyone else, learn that it was I who decided what was and wasn't a threat! Everyone was there at court to serve me, and whether it was for a brief or extended time was more than most of them deserved.

As time passed we held our breath as Cardinal Fleury showed every sign of approaching his end. I was thirty-three when he died, after fighting a long battle until the last moment, and serving me for seventeen years. I mourned him with honest tears, when I'd gotten everything from this man whom I'd come to see as a father. Gratitude filled me for his sound management that had resulted in economic prosperity and political stability. But could I maintain it all on my own? Like Louis XIV, I shunned the idea of another minister, and had a growing wish to rule given my proper age. My respect for Cardinal Fleury only deepened in light of all the warring factions at court, among them the partisans of Chauvelin, of Belle-Isle, of Tencin, of Maurepas, of the Duc de Richelieu, and the ancient clans of Orléans and Condé.

This increasingly complex situation that seemed to leave us at an impasse so intimidated and frustrated me that I often wished it would implode on itself. Why did everyone else, especially the English, seem to be getting on better than us? In our age of literary-philosophic salons, I wanted to prove the naysaying writers and philosophers that our complex system was both reflective of and effective in employing rationality and precision to enhance our decisions. Cardinal Fleury's often stringent economic calculations resurfaced, and I couldn't help but fear they'd become an even bigger concern with the ongoing War of Austrian Succession, unwanted by the Cardinal.

Worst of all, I feared most the public's growing discontent, who gossiped and created libelous poems of my relations with the Mailly-Nesle sisters. Would throwing them all in the Bastille resolve the matter of their blatant *lèse-majesté*, or, on the contrary, fuel their hateful disrespect? Despite the crushing weight of their expressed hate of my weakness, I instead tried to see it as an unspoken, even playful, contractual exchange of our mutual disappointments. Amidst my unrelenting concerns, I knew I could show them that I was not just a hunting and pleasure-loving spectator in my own kingdom.

Relieved by Cardinal Fleury's disappearance, I noticed Marie Anne's deepening interest in politics, while she feigned indifference and voiced interest in the candidates she knew I favored, like d'Argenson and Noailles. Whatever power she thought she'd have over me I trust I set her in place in my way, that day when she tried to snatch a letter out of my hand. I instantly tossed the letter in the fire, though it had occurred to me to push her in the flames first. There were too many times when I was certain her games were worse than anything men could come up with. But I played along, and let her think me the pliant lover in the palm of her hand. Yet the fun was mine when I had my favorite machinist Arnoult build the flying chair for her to visit more discreetly, while she'd arrogantly assume it was for lovesick convenience.

Consumed by this familiar deluge of change within and around me, I was torn between wanting to control it and watch it unfurl. Could God really have given me all these desires for me to ignore and reject them all? Weren't we allowed to taste some of them to truly learn and better understand what it meant? Perhaps I was still a child, perpetually unsure, and though the philosophers praised this new age of guilt-less pleasure, I didn't think that I could ever reach it—or that

I even wanted to. There might be a pleasure separated from God, but I tried to take it as a good sign that even I wasn't depraved enough to want that.

But a more frightening prospect came to me. Was I a kind of mutant who, aside from my chest scar, showed no physical signs, yet was irreparably misshapen and deformed inside? In Ovid's *Metamorphoses*, Salmacis, the naiad, rejected the ways of Diana for vanity and idleness. When one day Hermaproditus bathed in her pool, she fell in love with him, but he rejected her. In revenge for his rejection, she pleaded to the gods who answered her call to never leave him by fusing them together as a deity with male and female parts.

I recalled the peculiar painting by de Troy, who'd painted my beloved *Hunting Meal* and had since relocated as Director of the French Academy in Rome. In it, they were both nude, with Hermaphroditus gazing to the sky for help, while Salmacis reached up to him, her robust form as if stronger than his.

What if I'd been bathed in, or even drank, water cursed by Hermaphroditus to suffer the same fate, unbeknownst to me? If the Turkish embassy of Effendi Mehmed Said had somehow succeeded, during their recent visit, in giving me some of its water from the fountain in his lands, I wouldn't know of it. I reassured myself that it was unlikely when this visit promised the wished-for Turkish assistance to France against Austria. Neither was he like Moulay Ismail, that tyrannical Moroccan Sultan who'd urged Louis XIV to convert to Islam, and who enslaved captured Christians that included some from our lands.

More gossip spread through Paris of the visit of a white moor, whose traits resembled that of his Negro race, except that his hair, eyelashes, and skin were of striking lightness. While some saw them as inferior, others said they were proud of their obvious divine favor displayed by their distinct and rare appearance. At first it saddened, then disgusted me yet again, that no matter a man's origin, it seemed his treatment often had to be the extremes of either the worst or the best, as if it couldn't be sufficient to treat them like a person. I thought of my youngest Louise, away at Fontevraud with her sisters, whose small form had worried us and had come to include a crooked spine that affected her gait, and prayed for her to remain in God's loving care.

I did occasionally come to wonder about my fourth daughter, the feisty eleven-year old Adélaïde. The favorite of the Queen, at six years old, she'd thrown herself at my feet, begging to stay rather than go off to Fontevraud with her sisters, and to which I yielded. One morning, with some golden *louis* in her pocket, she'd taken it upon herself to lead the army and fight the English, whose king she wanted to bring at my feet. Inspired by her reading of the holy texts, she would do like Judith and offer herself to them and, honored by her person, she'd kill them one after the other. While others sought to reprimand this base and even cruel feeling in her, I was grateful that her innocence sheltered her from its true meaning, while being impressed with her clearly developing fire. She certainly didn't get it from her mother, and I prided myself that some of it had to come from me, and that she even secretly sensed my consternation with the English.

For obvious reasons of state security, she could not know that we had already begun plans to descend on Britain and assist in the Jacobite cause of the beloved Charles Edward Stuart to regain his grandfather's throne for his father James. The prospect of this heroic feat of restoring the House of Stuart and turning Britain into our client state was tempting, while I doubted all along our ability and boldness of going against our powerful foe who challenged our presence at our colonies all over the world.

That fire finally burned enough in me too, and, recalling the Maréchal de Noailles's brief text of thirty-three suggestions, I resolved to take personal command of our troops fighting at the War of Austrian Succession. Even my cousin the Prince de Conti had early on attached himself to Belle-Isle's and the Marquis de Maillebois's armies, in defiance of my ban on Princes of the Blood partaking in active military service. That I sincerely hoped for his success did not mean I didn't want some of my own.

I gently declined the Queen's pleading to come along, citing the prohibitive costs, and after some words to my pious Catholic *dévot* Dauphin and a letter to *maman* Ventadour, requesting her prayers, I was off to my beloved troops. In the midst of my bravery—which I knew shocked others as much as it did me—I was blessed in the summer with the unexpected arrival of my haughty Marie Anne, with her sister Diane Adélaïde. I flattered myself that my attention and favors surpassed her fears of the real dangers of such an undertaking. If she wanted to finally put herself at my service in this dire moment, why should I refuse? Despite her insistence to follow me, I initially left her behind during campaigns, but I eventually yielded to her wish, and henceforth our apartments were kept close to each other's. And what of it, if the gossip of austere Catholics spread at the scandal of having her there? I hadn't summoned her, and wasn't her thick flesh a fitting reward—and a trifle—in light of all that this brave French king was doing for his people!

When she fell sick at Reims, I couldn't help but be filled with a dark delight that perhaps she'd learn her lesson and go back, granting me this victory to myself rather than her dispensable charms. She of the cold calculating heart might've already forgotten her sister Pauline Félicité, but I never would, and I hoped that she was understanding this, even as she'd never admit it. I feigned anguish at her state, and for the first time I saw how pretending to be stressed could actually be a relief from the real thing! In guise of precaution, I spoke of her burial and her mausoleum, knowing I would not have it surpass in glory to that of Pauline Félicité's. Happily for her, she quickly recovered and, having delayed our troop's departure for just a day, we continued on our way to Metz.

Whatever doubts I'd had about Marie Anne's cunning harmful influence on me was confirmed when I soon fell sick at Metz. I, who had outlived my parents, brother, and two children, now had to return to death's door in the midst of my glorious victories! Yet I fought it, and enjoyed the overwhelming torment as each day the two camps—that of my mistress on one side, and those of the pious Catholic *dévots* on the other—fretted over their fates, should my life end. Which side should I have chosen, when a king surpasses his subjects?

Was my surgeon La Peyronie siding with my mistress the indication of where I should lean? Or had I, in my familiar insecurity and eagerness to turn to others for answers, placed too much faith in him and his so-called medical knowledge? Given my feverish stupor, he'd even called other doctors from the region, including two Jews. In my delirium, I mused that even these learned men could be as clueless as I, and that I should be the subject in that moment was more fitting than they could ever know. I thought of my proud kin the Prince de Conti, whose name I'd recently toasted in honor of his own victories in Piedmont.

I knew that Marie Anne feared most the humiliation of having to be renounced as my mistress and banished from court, as possible condition for my receiving absolution for my sins. How delightful, when she should've thought of that before involving herself in my life! Suspended between life and death, I half wanted to stay there, but the time had come to choose. And confession it was, because Marie Anne certainly was not worth my eternal damnation.

She and Diane Adélaïde were ordered to leave my side, and given their slowness in acquiescing, I was convinced to order their express departure from the city to hasten my soul's recovery. I imagined that they would have trouble finding a carriage, and that it would fuel their fear of the peasants who sang their disapproval in verses and song from village to village. I trust that she felt my wrath as I mentally reminded them that it was nothing compared to what Pauline Félicité's body had suffered.

Yet the greedy clergy wanted more, and had I been in full health I'm nearly certain that I would've denounced their manipulations once and for all! I saw then, in the throes of sickness, how pain might give you a kind of deepened perception. I'd never been so keen on the philosophers, but what if it was true that some clergy—Catholic,

Protestant, Jansenist, Masonic, and who knew what else—didn't mind to entrap believers with their own machinations? What if—and this was cruelest and perhaps most delightful of all—they were all wrong and despite my flaws I'd been allowed to glimpse through this! And if it was wrong, and even blasphemous for me to question and think this, was my ultimate surrender not the proof of my concern for my soul—separating me from mere beast!—when I accepted to a public repentance? I pushed through the weight of all the criticism I'd already faced, and though I did not wish to be hated, and even selfishly wanted to be loved, my confession had to be for God first, and who now seemed so different from too many who often claimed to serve and represent Him.

To my shock, the burden lifted off as I confessed what I never thought I would: that I was unworthy of being called the Most Christian King. I asked God's and my subjects' forgiveness for the scandal and the bad example I had set, hating myself yet wishing that such vile traits might not follow me in the beyond by leaving them here. Though I hadn't yet wanted to go, perhaps it was for the best, when I'd leave having fought for my kingdom, and I might see Pauline Félicité again, along with my children, parents, and sibling.

If possible, I wanted to see the Queen, the Dauphin, and my daughters one last time, so I had them come separately and stay nearby. The Queen embraced me as I slept and I knew our love would never fully die when my heart swelled with tenderness at her honest tearful emotion—so rare in our courtly life. I wanted to be as equally touched when my fourteen-year-old Dauphin arrived unexpectedly—coaxed by his governor—but I couldn't approve his carelessness that could've put his life in danger and jeopardized the throne of France. Nor could I rejoice to suspect that he believed he might succeed me shortly. Worst of all, I hated to think he might partially approve of the spiritual manipulations I'd just suffered through.

I had feared hell for so long, and always would, but I glimpsed then, too, how much love my fickle subjects could still display. If nothing else, didn't we have our mercurial moods in common? As my end loomed, masses rang out throughout the kingdom; emotions and concern overtook their lives as it did mine. Protestants and Jews prayed for me, and churches stayed open at night in Paris. Too late I thought, if I were to survive, I would've liked to build a church in honor of Saint Geneviève, the patron saint of Paris who'd diverted Attila's Huns away from the city in the fifth century.

I was not finished, because though hunted, wounded, and prepared for eternal mounting on the wall, I lived. I'd come so close to the end, and though I couldn't explain it, I'd been chosen to keep the hunt going; another confirmation that I wasn't as fragile as I—and others—had thought. Back on the road, I made stops on the way home, and was cheered wherever I went, topped with my triumphant return to Paris, acclaimed as *le Bien-Aimé*, the "well-loved" conqueror king who gave up his lover and returned to virtue. Even as I doubted its appearance, I thought my heart would explode then, from such display of love that I not only didn't expect, but didn't deserve.

Amidst my grotesque revival, how could I be blamed for seeing my life as but a charade of endless happiness and pain? Why was I tormented by sickness, and maybe even worthy of death, only to be rescued out of it? For I returned home to none other than news that our seventh daughter Thérèse had died at Fontevraud of smallpox. In her eight years, I hadn't seen her in six, since she'd left to what was meant to be her temporary abode. The Queen, in her faith's consolation that she was meant to suffer, once more resigned herself, while I drifted between tearful grief, anger, and even gratitude. Had it been her life for mine? Though I could be judged heartless, God knows I not only mourned every child's death with a pain that each time took a piece of me away, but also had to endure it under a mask of steel endurance.

I tried to drown my surging cruel thoughts that I might outlive all my children with as much food and Champagne as I could. Given the celebrations, it was thought best to keep the news quiet to avoid dampening the French spirits with another lost princess. Her pure soul had surely gone to its reward while I told myself the French deserved their moment of rejoicing. In our failure to see her, and her siblings, I forced myself not to wish that she was buried closer, when she deserved to be in the grounds she'd most known in her short life. At least she had the notable Plantagenets Eleanor of Aquitaine, King Henri II of Britain, and their son Richard the Lionheart for companions.

My second night in Paris I went to the Queen's door and scratched three times, though if she did eventually answer, I'd already gone. Surely I'd let myself romanticize in thinking that in her grief and own fragile health I could lend her some of mine, and prove it with another healthy child... Until I realized I didn't think I could've taken another rejection from her, especially so soon after having recovered.

In my whirling sense of loss and selfish indifference, nothing was easier than to call Marie Anne back—they'd been mistreated too, even if I didn't care much about it—and I could restore her place. And though it surely flattered her vanity, I hoped it was also a fitting hint that I didn't care for the clergy who'd exceeded their authority by forcing it out of me for their own benefit. As for my subjects' potential dissatisfaction, I was sure the love they'd already shown me was enough to sustain me.

The hunt would go on, and hunt her down I did with all the proof of my rejuvenated health. The stag-king ran: struck into her flesh, slicing deep enough to make her scream out her feigned indifference that I skillfully choked with timely squeezes of her neck. After all she'd put me through, I'd decide how she'd breathe, and all the better if the terror lingered in her widened eyes for anyone, or even just me, to recognize.

A survivor in my own kingdom, I thought of the wild girl Marie-Angélique again, as much from my growing interest as in the satisfaction of it displeasing Marie Anne. I was touched by the pious Louis, Duc d'Orléans's care for her in taking her under his permanent protection and moving her to a convent in Paris, in preparation for taking the veil. There was envy, too. This evolved son of the Regent—who'd had his trysts with opera actresses, had represented me at the proxy marriage ceremony with the Queen at Strasbourg, and who'd been next in line to the throne until my son was born—had found solace in devotion after the death of his wife from childbirth, the year after my own wedding. He'd since retired at the Abbey of Sainte-Geneviève built by Clovis, where he spent his time translating Biblical texts, using his wealth for charitable causes, and protecting men of science.

At times, his religious fervor impressed and intimidated me even more than Cardinal Fleury's, with his theology education and Oriental language learning that fired up his Bible reading. He was so confident that none died, and that souls took other forms that my child-like fascination and wish for solace shrank before my sullying guilt. Why hadn't I reached that unshakeable place myself? Why wasn't I strong enough to renounce my excesses and return to my Queen, even if only for a chaste union?

Then again, if it was my punishment to only feel its temporary grace, then why should I reject what God gave me, including my mistresses for my earthly needs? Marriage changes things, and surely I had not expected that my Queen would turn me away. Even he might've become a different person, if he'd instead married one of the suggested daughters of Tsar Peter the Great, Anna—or my previous contender—Elizabeth of Russia. All the same, with his good and charitable nature, he was one of the few of whom I was certain harbored no resentment at my rejection of his son marrying my Henriette years before.

While my name was expected to be known elsewhere, Marie-Angélique's story had since gathered such attention as to spread to Britain and Sweden. I struggled between wanting to see her for myself and keeping the image of her I had in mind untainted. Having learned our language, manners, and Catholic faith, I considered visiting the convent to compliment her on that achievement, if only to see her reaction.

I imagined she would make an incomparable sight, as I watched this unique runaway—who might've lived among the Indians or even at our prized Antilles colony—demurely doing her needlework in her pious attire. Was she wondering at the pointless endeavor, or was she instead grateful for it, as she imagined skinning a rabbit or some other creature? She'd look up and smile innocently at me, aware and even pleased that we saw through each other's facades. But sometimes that seemed too much to bear, and I preferred to think of her as Eve wandering in her garden that she'd somehow lost.

I'd even flirted with the idea of inviting her to Versailles, and if her presence at court would shock many, I delighted in thinking of Marie Anne's unease most of all. Ultimately I decided against turning Marie-Angélique as an exotic curiosity, and preferred to have her kept away from our golden cage of vipers, even if I suspected they were no match for her.

My curiosity and thirst for knowledge ignited, I wanted to know what she did to fight her lurking desire for blood, and why—so it was said—it was strongest when she looked at a child. Surely the pious Duc d'Orléans, who'd been as fascinated by the Indian embassy as I was, would think me mad if I wanted one of Marie-Angélique's teeth. Just a single, lonely one... among all the others she sadly lost after taking on our diet that weakened her health. Or some of her fingernails, and which, unlike others who'd have them as mere monstrous trinkets, I'd appreciate as precious tokens of all she'd endured. I'd tell her that I—and I alone!—understood her dislike for social gatherings, and even her dislike of being touched. For if nothing else when I thought of the wild girl—whose true name had vanished, or had been kept secret to herself—I shared her reluctance, if not at times raging hate for human company. I considered asking the Duc d'Orléans what he'd think about this aspect of our personalities, and decided he might forgive it in her, but not in me.

Though I considered Marie-Angélique no beast, by then I had begun hearing of such a new one. It came in the form of a young, multi-talented married beauty named Jeanne Antoinette. Connected to financiers, she had an estate near Sénart and cleverly drew attention to herself while I hunted. When I smugly mentioned to Marie Anne that I'd gifted Jeanne Antoinette a venison, her condescending tone delightfully betrayed her own fearfully fragile position. Only a few months later she fell sick and died, and all the better she hadn't given me children, because if she had I wasn't sure I'd keep my early promise to recognize them. When it was suggested to undertake her burial at night—to avoid what had happened with Pauline Félicité—I almost violently protested until, in my perpetual goodness and wish to be finished with it, I relented.

Much more devastating to me was the death of *maman* Ventadour six days later. What a good, strong mother she'd been, when her ninety years doubled the average lifespan! Surely more than anyone, her prayers had kept me alive during the campaign, and at least she'd seen me return as a beloved king.

As ever, I soothed my ailing soul by soaring along the forest of Sénart, thinking of the Queen and Pauline Félicité but also, for the first time, of forging a new path in unknown terrain.

I welcomed the opportunity to shift attention to my son's affairs, and negotiated his marriage with the Infanta Maria Teresa Rafaela of Spain. At nineteen, she was three years older than him, and the younger sister of Mariana Victoria and my son-in-law, Philip. Despite our differences, it had to be a splendid affair for my son, as it'd been with his older sister Elisabeth's marriage to the Infante Philip. The wedding was held at the royal chapel of Versailles, complete with its dazzling wedding procession and a comedy-ballet by Rameau, *The Princess of Navarre.*

My dalliance with Diane Adélaïde at its end, I was myself a reborn young, free spirit yearning to partake in the joy and rush of the endless festive dinners, balls, ballets, and plays that stretched on for days. It was a new future for my son, and also for myself. Since it was also Carnaval, I found it fitting to indulge myself and the guests with several masked balls; tinged with that Venetian pleasure that allowed for all manner of society to interact with less concern for etiquette.

My favorite was the Yew Tree Ball; where throngs of attendees clustered, as if come from all corners of the world in their festive colorful and jeweled attires, and predictably poised to knock aside any barriers in their way. Disguised as a yew tree, I hunted, floating among the cackling-sweet madness, tempering my Champagne drinking before its time. The Queen was in her white dress sown with pearls, while the Dauphin was a shepherd and his wife the Dauphine a flower girl, while I relished that everyone wondered where I was. Strengthened by the memory of Pauline Félicité and I at the ball six years before, I spotted my prey, and approached Diana the huntress, who'd already sacrificially put herself in my path before, while I hunted.

Would it have been better if I'd died at Metz? Would I have still made the same choice if I'd known what would come from it? Such was the Beast; born Jeanne Antoinette Poisson. The much-vaunted, oh-so flawless Jeanne Antoinette had all the gifts that a perfect woman could wish for: beauty, education, wit, taste, musical talent. Surely among the most beautiful women a man had ever seen! And yet, something in her polished, amateur manner awakened in me a curious mix of tenderness tinged with pity and repugnance. With all her gifts, this non-noble bourgeoise's highest goal of having me still required my royal agreement.

I like to think I'd seen through that mask of sickening, so-called perfection, and wanted to shatter and shake things up, let the raging shower of bloody cards, feathers, and limbs fall where it may. Because though I'd often thought that danger should be fled, and war avoided, in her I saw a way of owning and observing the Beast.

I could imagine the court's deafening gasps and protests at the thought of a mere common bourgeoise as my new favorite, and that added to my delightfully burgeoning hunger. Did they not see it? How could a king be soiled, and by a non-noble at that! I had the royal blood, and she had the money needed by France through her financier family. What time was there to lose? She'd realized her violent love for me after my sickness at Metz—though she was pregnant then and birthed a daughter soon after—and after years of seeing me through her window before driving her phaeton my way. She'd had to work her way up, and though everyone would think this a temporary dalliance unworthy of my station, the prospect of her—or should I say, France's—money in return for having her as my mistress was too good to pass up. As the king, chosen by God, I would do my best, and even lend her freedom in certain affairs. And if—and when—things went to hell, then it ultimately wouldn't be my doing when in her cold porcelain hands.

I let her inherent inferiority complex cloaked in good, graceful manners worship me in all her rather mediocre abilities. How could such a one, with an uncertain father and libertine mother whose reputation caused scandal, be so cold and wanting in bed? She didn't have to smell like roses, lavender, or bergamot, but even the sought-after musk and ambergris aphrodisiac perfumes she'd doused herself in were nothing in comparison to Pauline Félicité natural raw scent. Is that all her gifts resulted in? It took much of my strength not to burst into laughter, half wondering if she'd paid off all these gossips to spread the good word about her. She was the prime example of the peacock with all the talents, except for the one men most wanted her—and especially her kind—for.

And yet, I tasted this strange new pleasure of letting one of such lower rank surrender herself to me, and in my hunger I thrust harder, lodging in her marbled corpse my denigrating reprimand. If that was what some libertines meant when they took pleasure in humiliating others, I thought some of it was beginning to make sense. What fool did she take me for? In my grace I said nothing of my suspicion that some of her reluctance was as much from her frigid nature, as from some ailment she might've caught from past encounters. That I had the best physicians did not decrease my disappointment—and caution—in this whole affair.

Before officially granting all my genuine promises, I left her with qualified men in charge of educating her on our refined courtly ways, and to let her finalize her separation from her husband at my request. Thus I let her yearning for me grow as I rejoined the Flemish war front in Tournai. With my son the Dauphin, Maurice, the Maréchal de Saxe, and our army, we triumphed against the Duke of Cumberland's army at Fontenoy. But our glory did not lessen the losses, an important lesson I made sure to remind my proud *dévot* son. I made no secret that our success came from God, and the skill of Maurice de Saxe and the officers who'd led brave regiments to this happy end. For the first time, I flattered myself that my brave presence in the midst of battle might've also inspired them to push on for a long desired victory against the English.

The news soon spread and Jeanne Antoinette's new favor with me reached Voltaire—whom she knew as a *salonnière*—and who soon wrote a celebratory poem in my honor, *The Battle of Fontenoy*. Though the man's satirical pen had already earned him time in the Bastille and multiple occasions to flee, I did not mind our victory celebrated by one of the most famous writers in France and Europe.

I returned to Paris with the Dauphin, feasted with the Queen and my daughters collectively called Mesdames, and plunged into the welcoming arms of Jeanne Antoinette. To my surprise, it was easy to be filled with a kind of tenderness I'd last truly felt with Pauline Félicité, so I reigned in my fervor to the echoes of my acclaiming people and exalting *Te Deum* of Fontenoy, and other blissful hymns that filled the kingdom. Thankfully, Jeanne Antoinette appeared more enthusiastic this time, so I indulged her as she went on about the popular novel *La Belle et la Bête* by Madame de Villeneuve, about a young prince who was cast under a spell. Turned into a beast, his spell could only be broken with true love, which he finds with la Belle. Ignoring any potential hints, I took it as another reference to her circle of literary friends, for the author was the mistress of her previous drama coach, and royal censor, Crébillon.

And lest she think she was the source of inspiration for our victory rather than the money to fund the troops, I teased her that it was part of our agreement for her to keep me satisfyingly entertained no matter the state of affairs. As we both knew, she'd also yet to be introduced at court, so it was in her best interest to deliver the finest that she could to keep my attention.

Surely emboldened by our successes, I was just as pleased that my son the Dauphin had finally overcome his shy nature—mirrored by his wife's—by consummating their union and quashing any lingering suspicions of impotence. How could I tell him that I was proud of him? I dared not tell him that, despite the famous saying of seven times the first night, it had also actually taken me time to consummate with his mother at about the same age. My pure, untouched, glorious, Jesuit-loving *dévot* son, loved and seen by his sisters as the ideal Christian prince. Would he hate me even more, if he knew how I'd been weakened and soiled as a boy? Hating to even admit it to myself, its evil hold seemed as if forever fixed on me, and though I failed consistently, I tried to fight it off in my way. If he didn't already, he'd think me weak and pathetic, and in my selfishness I didn't want to add to that. I wanted him to have as good a life as a French prince could have, and though our circumstances with my mistresses repulsed him, at least he had his parents and siblings alive to shower him with their love.

I knew I had to savor the moment, and try I did, for I suspected I would never again surpass these momentary comparisons to the Sun King. As if proof of that, it soon after came to me that a certain troubling publication required my attention. Not only was a fairy tale named *Tanastès* circulating, but it was shockingly traced down to mademoiselle Marie Bonafon, residing in Versailles in service to the Princess of Montauban, in league with the *dévots*.

The puzzle-like story, whose style had been popularized by La Fontaine and La Bruyère, employed other names that could be matched to actual people in my courtly entourage. I could hardly believe the audacity of putting in print and circulating the private matters of Versailles, and especially of Marie Anne and myself at Metz, along with her return, and my new choice of mistress.

I vacillated between disbelief and disgust. Had she really written it alone, or had she, most likely, been coaxed to the task by a self-serving noble? Just as alarming was ensuring that no traces of it would remain, when an underground network seemed to link Versailles, Paris, and Rouen—and who knew where else. It seemed impossible that others wouldn't follow, if inspired by such an initial bold attempt.

And yet even I couldn't deny that part of it intrigued me. In a sense, it was a clever idea to have the child king Tanastès snatched away by a sylph, while my evil lustful look-alike Agamil ruled in my place. How often did I feel like multiple people in one body all seeking different things! In it were references to the Queen—and an eventual reconciliation with her—Louise Julie, Marie Anne, and Diane Adélaïde, but none of Pauline Félicité! In many ways, and because she'd also left me Charles, even if he lived away and I didn't see him, that felt most unforgivable of all.

Did I have to remind my subjects that their opinions were not free of consequences, or did they simply not care anymore? It dampened any fragile sense of triumph I'd had, and as I tried to decipher the moment that had sealed my fate in their eyes, I reluctantly settled on Metz. That damning confession: surely this text wouldn't even exist if my private confession hadn't been publicized to fuel my subjects' rejection of me! But how dare they presume to judge my royal person! What did they know of my burden! How often do people, in their wisdom, have endless criticisms but no solutions, or only selfish ones that benefit themselves and wash themselves of the responsibility by pleading innocence or fleeing when it fails!

Perhaps I'd been too light in my approach thus far, when not long before a libertine novel anonymously titled *The Sofa* had been traced to its origin in the son of Crébillon. The author's punishment had been an exile of thirty leagues from Paris, and even the later claim that it'd been published against his will—and better yet, commissioned by Frederick II of Prussia—surely were convenient lies to allow him to return. But even that silly tale did not breach inside the private walls of Versailles, to potentially inspire others to do the same. As such, off to the Bastille went Marie Bonafon, an outcome that should serve as harsher deterrent.

I found amusement in Jeanne Antoinette's anticipated day of introduction to court, henceforth titled Marquise de Pompadour. She moved into the apartment previously inhabited by Marie Anne and Diane Adélaïde—with its stunning view over the forest of Marly—and became part of my private *petits soupers* in my *petits cabinets*, where only my closest saw me as my most relaxed. She sat for Nattier as Diana the huntress in commemoration of our meeting, and lest she get any ideas while enjoying my kindness, I did not let her forget that I was the one in charge. It was all the more necessary in case she had some occult Masonic powers—as side effect from her financial connections—that allowed her to occasionally glimpse into my thoughts. When she suggested I give attention to the Queen, I feigned reluctant acquiescence because I'd already been thinking of doing so, but feared upsetting her too soon. After all, the Queen was also worthy of my generosity, when Cardinal Fleury had so often restrained it, and perhaps especially when I showered châteaux and other lavish gifts on my mistress.

My dislike of that ugly-nosed Voltaire was cemented with Rameau's opera-ballet, *The Temple of Glory*, whose libretto he wrote. Meant to celebrate our victory at Fontenoy, he pompously thought he'd flatter me by painting me as Trajan, as though an enlightened despot forgiving of his enemies. I seethed at his snide vanity and suggestion that not only was I unworthy of Glory, but that I should exchange it for a Temple of Happiness to gift the world instead. Me, give the world happiness, when I could hardly give it to myself! Even if I often questioned my own worth, he so surpassed his place that it took all my strength not to send him back to the Bastille. How easily and arrogantly he hid behind his mask of self-righteousness while he conveniently enriched himself amidst our wars! I made it clear to Jeanne Antoinette that his presence would be limited and there would be no further overreaching machinations from him through her help.

Unsurprisingly, Jeanne Antoinette's enemies at court increased, and though the Queen soon took kindly to her—with Jeanne Antoinette's efforts of respectful surrender—the Maréchal de Richelieu, the Prince de Conti, Mesdames and the Dauphin were among them. Not only did that not bother me, but in some ways it even pleased me. If, in her feigned gentle nature, it was sometimes more than the Beast could bear, I had no need to remind her that she'd wanted into my world. Though I didn't particularly care about any pains of hers on that account, she surprised us all with her lack of viciousness and refusal to have others do so in her apartments.

Surely she'd learned to wear the mask well, for if all this looked the portrait of perfection to everyone else, I suspected it only further concealed the wrath somewhere deep within her. My mistress of pleasures: meant to entice with all the senses, and enough to foolish most, but not all. What did it look like—I both wondered and dreaded, hating that hers being worse than mine might reflect well on me for once, while posing a larger danger to France. A twisted pleasure grew in me, that while this lurking huntress had marked me for years, I might've also been secretly assigned as her captor to closely watch and limit her movements in my kingdom.

I noticed Jeanne Antoinette's deepening boredom at my private *soupers* and comet card games, and I increasingly took to Champagne to add some excitement to our trysts. If she thought she was keeping me excited with her prudish ways, it was having the opposite effect. Even if it was our success in war that had rekindled the fire of devotion and duty in me, she would've been just as displeased if I told her it only made me love my Queen even more, despite our distance. Even my pious Queen had shown more enthusiasm in her motherly role, and had ultimately rejected me due to her doctor's recommendations.

I might be forced to endure that from my wife—who'd given me many children, after all—but a mistress was laughable and pitiful. The thought of endless money as my solace to our stability, I let its hideous golden molten form, with antlers on its head and at each shoulder serving as arms, wrap me in its stinking rotten egg embrace. My head spun for hours, as I imagined what it might've been like to die covered by ash or eaten by lava, as oblivious Pompeii and Herculaneum had suffered.

Maurice de Saxe brought us another victory with the bold winter siege of Brussels, news that we welcomed along with the Jacobite rising's recent successes that had lured some of the English army back home. Though it had taken us some time to acquire victories, I thought I could begin to get used to them.

While I could enjoy some of Jeanne Antoinette's company and dedication—if not need—to keep me continually entertained, at times I think she enjoyed the honor more than I. She was constantly with me in my travels, and though at first it bothered me to notice her boredom at the hunts—another sign of her duplicity—I soon enjoyed thinking that it was a small fitting punishment. But even incessant entertainment becomes redundant and boring in its own way. As La Bruyère said, we're almost always bored with people with whom it is not allowed to be bored.

Her charade of lightness and ease seemed increasingly one of such skilled pretense that it looked natural to anyone flattered by vain courtly manners. Too many were all too willing to play along in hopes of gaining her favor and potentially reaching their own wished-for rank.

She had such endless ideas of collecting glassware, silver, Gobelins tapestries, silks, chandeliers, marbles, and porcelain designs… Not to mention fawning over Boucher's idyllic paintings with classical or pastoral scenes; soft and airy renderings to cast away dullness with her forced creativity and need for gaiety that at times it nearly made me sick. How I wished I might overcome my natural shyness then, so that

I might throw up on her and add a splash of rawness from the pit of my royal constipated hell!

Where were her messy raging tears for her son lost as an infant, or even a fiery unrepentance for leaving her passionately enamored husband for me? That as the king I was the obvious choice of women did not mean she had to be so heartlessly light and indifferent, especially since he was not my competition.

By then well aware of her feigned interest in hunting to catch my initial attention, I did not tell her that I had much more lurid images in mind than my growing collection of bizarre stag antlers paintings. Instead, I mused that should the need ever arise, I could threaten—and truly provide!—her with horrifying hunting scenes to replace her bucolic painless dreams. She might be the eager patron of the arts, obsessed with attention and public spectacle, but she would only reflect one idealistic and overtly feminine part.

As I wavered in my love-hate for her, I recalled that I could very well do as I please, be free in my leanings and provoke with my innermost visions—my mind a living cabinet of horrific curiosities! That's what libertines engaged in like demons, this proud display of unabashed filth that they claimed set them free. But they were not free—and I wasn't sure if it was worse that they didn't know it, or knew it and kept on deceiving! As she'd already shown me, they were masks, and bad ones at that, and though Versailles etiquette required the monitoring of our emotions, in reality I was not one of them. Philosophers, writers, and scientists might even praise my far-seeing evil eye—or a few of them might even understand—but I did not need their praise when sharing such a secret seemed a blasphemous breaching of the sacred.

I knew the great power of images and words to influence, which is why I did not create, let alone share them to lead others astray. That she would go so far as to fashion and dwell in a world where only "happiness" was allowed seemed an even deeper madness than mine, and with which I could never fully reconcile. Would art always continue to deceive in plain sight, and was it, like Jeanne Antoinette herself, part of its twisted charm? Even as king, I couldn't be the only one to know that her pastel euphoria was incomplete.

In my frustration with Jeanne Antoinette, God saw fit to remind me of the blessings I had in my midst in the form of my daughters. It was not from boredom but from sincerity that I began spending more time with Henriette and Adélaïde, who joined me weekly for the hunt, to excursions to Choisy and la Muette, and to my private *petits soupers*.

I marveled at how I could father such different creatures. At nineteen, the younger twin Henriette had a gentle melancholic nature that found refuge and solace in her viola music, which thrived from lessons by the gifted Jean-Baptiste Forqueray. The fourteen-year old witty Adélaïde had long displayed a headstrong character, with a great passion for learning through reading, painting, and calculus. Her ephemeral dark-eyed beauty had not gone unnoticed though I wondered how a contender—if any worthy of her rank should appear—might fare in the face of such tenacity. They were fond of their brother the Dauphin, and all shared their dislike for Jeanne Antoinette. I could not expect my children to understand my amorous need and choice of mistress, and despite their disapproval, it was a balm to know their reaction was in part in support of their mother whom they deeply loved.

In the whirlwind of scientific changes I heard of Jean-Antoine Nollet's curious experiment of electricity with a Leyden jar. Naturally I had to have a repeat of this performance at Versailles, where I amusedly marveled at the one hundred and eighty guards holding hands in the Hall of Mirrors, and jumping at the same time as the electric charge pulsed through them.

Less delightfully shocking were the news of Bonnie Prince Charlie's defeat at Culloden, a crushing blow after months of victorious campaigning. His loyal supporters still had much fire in them, and I tried to envision the future as we awaited the birth of the Dauphin's first child, the second time I would be a grandfather. In the summer came a granddaughter, Marie Thérèse, though three days later her mother was dead. My good, dutiful son, who'd formed a deep bond with his equally shy, red-haired wife, was left broken-hearted. I wanted my poor Dauphin, widowed at sixteen, to grieve his beloved, as I'd grieved Pauline Félicité, and yet we both knew of his need to secure an heir by remarrying promptly.

Maurice de Saxe soon suggested Maria Josepha of Saxony, supported by Jeanne Antoinette in the view of changing our antagonistic relations with Saxony and expanding and enhancing our foreign affairs. Naturally, I didn't let on my initial reluctance, when Maria Josepha's grandfather Augustus II had deposed Stanislas, the Queen's father, from the Polish throne. The Queen would surely disapprove this match, and the Dauphin further pushed into resentment at this decision. Was it the Beast getting her shrewd revenge at the Dauphin and his now deceased wife's open hostility to her? And would this change things for the better, if indeed, she even aspired to that at all? But the other contenders would not do, the Queen relented, and so the news were announced, as the Dauphin wavered between apathy and persistent tearful misery. His near worshipping of her in death seemed as excessive as it was familiar in my unpredictable longing for Pauline Félicité.

For the wedding, Maria Josepha wore a glistening gown of gold and silver, which did little to add to her and her betrothed's downcast countenance. The celebrations—ovations, fireworks, canon blasts, *comédie-ballet*, ball, and banquet—were easily the most depressing I'd ever witnessed, shrouded in the heavy cloud of my son's dejection that I knew all too well. I hated that I could be so understanding of, yet helpless in his unhappy fate. But I dared not tell him that perhaps in time his pain would settle and he'd find a new, though never the same exact kind of happiness he'd had with his first wife. He might be afraid and confused, but I hoped that this movement, so unpredictable yet constant, could be to something other than doom.

But unfortunately he—and all of us—would have reason to remain morose, at least for a time, when soon after their Polish grandmother

Catherine Opalińska died, granting our customary change to mourning attire and décor for six months. I could hardly blame his morbid moods and games when, with his sisters, they took to locking themselves in the room of the departed Maria Teresa, surrounded by candles as they hid in the thick black curtains like ghosts, or laid on the floor and chanted, *We are dead! We are dead!*

To help ease his pain, I resolved to have another portrait done of his beloved first Dauphine, where she would stand out in an ermine-lined cloak adorned with fleur-de-lys, and an ornate gown of silver and gold amidst a beautifully darker background.

I took the opportunity to escape the dreary Versailles atmosphere by joining the troops of Maréchal de Saxe in Brussels to undertake the siege of Maastricht. Just the previous year I'd so rejoiced at his triumph in the city that I requested a *Te Deum* be sung at the cathedral Saint Gudule, until I'd happily rejoined the troops and attended yet another *Te Deum* at the same place, and lodged at the hotel d'Egmont. Though war could never be a painless endeavor, nor always transpire as expected, I could still try to placate the ever-lurking hate with negotiations. At the very least, we didn't ruthlessly bombard the city as Louis XIV had destructively done half a century before in 1695.

Returned from my three-month absence, Jeanne Antoinette soon after complained that the Dauphin, his wife, and his sisters decided to no longer speak to her. I reprimanded them for appearance's sake, but I secretly applauded their defiance and willingness to defend their mother and their principles. As much as Jeanne Antoinette did her best to maintain her cheerful appearance, I welcomed her own constant fears about my wavering interest in her, when her lack of passion for our intimacies was becoming a larger problem.

Whatever had happened to the Beast's violent love for me? Apparently it was not powerful enough to sustain its weak flame, when for her cold constitution she began following a warming diet of *chocolat* with triple doses of vanilla, truffle and celery soups, and crawfish. Amidst my tender caresses, it thoroughly satisfied me to secretly mock her and her deceptions, when I was nearly certain that it would prove as fruitful as her miscarriage. Likewise, I was confident that not even eating stag testicles would fix her. Thankfully I had my white, soft angora Brillant to wake me up in the morning, and whose company I increasingly preferred over hers.

She began collecting porcelain from Vincennes, and since I wanted portraits of all my children, which would also please the Queen, I sent Nattier to Fontevraud to paint my younger daughters in secret.

My life had been a whirlwind of uncertainties tinged with some victories, and yet the Devil's hold on me had not lessened, but instead increased. Harpies clung to my shoulders, whispering of mockery and curses—pamphlets, insults, secrets in... but no; secrets out! All of them—for the entire world to see!

*Imagine: the end of France!*

But that couldn't be! I retorted, surprised at my own defiance.

*In a sense, but let's say it did*, they challenged: what would I do, then? Would I finally repent?

*No! You are too weak*, the harpies sneered.

But it was just fear, just thoughts trying to overcome me! I tried to reassure myself, but the worst of it was that I knew they weren't entirely lying.

Had Jeanne Antoinette's own weakened health also gotten to me and infected me, and why hadn't I been more careful about it? In case she thought she was discreet, I'd heard of the green discharge she was producing, adding to my growing revulsion. It might explain that whiff of urine in her apartments—or dare I say her person—surely they played their part in fueling my nausea! At least my pious Queen, with all her faults, had never been with anyone else, let alone with any of ill-repute, to potentially pass me any of her venereal ailments.

While as the king, some mistakes were strictly mine, a part of me did not know how, or even really cared, to do anything about it. So what if in my fragile attempt at boldness after my triumph at Metz and Fontenoy, I'd overestimated myself with this mistress? I suspected the ever-lurking dangers, ready to strike at any moment, and yet I lived on, like a crowned puppet with limited ability—aware that it was ultimately out of my hands. Even this indifference wasn't enough, when dread paralyzed me with the sense of the worst mistake I'd made, one that I could hardly grasp or name, and would not be easily swept away.

My melancholy worsened when my son the Dauphin was struck by the tragedy of his first stillborn son. In our mourning, my fourth daughter Victoire turned fifteen and I eagerly granted her request to return home to Versailles, where her beauty and delicate manner was a balm to all our hearts. Though I was in no hurry to ponder her marriage, it pleased me that no contenders seemed suitable. Even the question of eventual matrimony for my youngest eleven-year old Louise, still at the Abbey, was met with her wish to be married to Jesus. Could it be; that sinful as I was, I'd taken part in making a child who genuinely wished to be one with God? I hid my unpredictable rattling emotion through my customary altered tone of voice, or even necessary throat-clearing, grateful that their purity had remained unscathed. How often I'd wondered that I might've been more pious, and better able to resist the powers of the flesh, if only I hadn't been bothered so young.

Touched and saddened to see my children growing and forming their own personalities and tastes despite our absence, I saw it as another instance of His grace that moved in mysterious ways. Victoire bonded with her mother, her sisters Henriette, Adélaïde, and brother the Dauphin, who encouraged her learning that had been neglected at the Abbey. Even sixteen-year-old Adélaïde, who'd begged to stay with me instead of joining her sisters, was a curious mix of wild beauty with a biting tinge of boyishness that continued to surprise me. Sometimes I wish they'd all followed her example and protested, and I would've simply had to say no to Cardinal Fleury on sending them away.

With her suitable age and beauty, Adélaïde had suitors, including the Prince de Conti, yet I selfishly shared her wish to remain unmarried rather than doing so beneath her station to one who was not a monarch or an heir to a throne. Besides, it was our secret that we collectively had other projects for him, and the thought of Adélaïde—had she been willing—potentially going away with him in due time did not please me.

For the second time that year, tragedy bitterly struck the Dauphin again, when his nearly two-year-old daughter Marie Thérèse from his first marriage died mysteriously, calling him to relapse into mourning for his first beloved wife. I wished I could take this pain from him, but all I could offer was my own familiar heartbreak over a dear, pure life cut short. That her death would not be officially mourned for being a princess under seven years of age was another rule whose cruelty I suspected he hated as much as I did. Our shattering silenced emotions were not enough to still the raging competing thoughts, for while he'd often blamed certain deaths and outcomes as retribution for my sins, what could he offer for explanation in his case? If he had his own secrets, perhaps he was beginning to learn of their unexpected, volatile weight, too.

It was in that 1748 year that Maurice Quentin de La Tour presented me—and the Salon—with my fuller pastel portrait, forever tinged with bitter-sweetness. One the one hand I remain struck by my indulgent confident gaze and posture adorned in ceremonial armor, while on the other there's a muted sadness with its multi-toned background suggesting the familiar, ever-looming melancholic storm. Just as he'd done three years before with an appealing, life-like sketch of my profile, he captures something of my better inner spirit with an aura of royal mystery that I can't help but praise.

There were also his pastels of the Queen, the Dauphin, and Maurice de Saxe, among others, but the boldest was the Queen's portrait by Nattier. In it, she sits in her striking red dress, her profile looking up in gentle contemplation as the Gospels lay open under her hand, as if piously glimpsing into the other world. Even as she reflects a simpler extraction than the court's preference, I marveled at this wife that had been assigned to me, at all the things I would've liked to say to her, but never would. I secretly smirked at the fact that even she was not sinless, given her unrepentant gluttony and her costly *cavagnole* gambling. As promised, there was also the endearing portrait of my son's departed first wife Maria Teresa, majestically sealed into our memories by Tocqué.

Jeanne Antoinette saw fit to sell some of her estates, and began building a new home on a broad plateau in Meudon, near the Seine and facing Sèvres, whose name of Bellevue fittingly suggested its beautiful views. I had the nauseating sense that she was once again doing too much, and not just because I wasn't used to seeing one of her rank be so frivolous with spending. Even if she was technically following protocol, it was no less annoyingly vain for her to emulate the nobles in spending—and regardless of income—to reinforce her image. Even with her financier family, didn't she ever worry about running out of funds? Whereas I'd once seen her—and some others'—constant need to spend as a sign of vivacity and benevolence, I had the growing sense of how wrong that was. For once, if my frugal tendencies born from concern made me appear a simple peasant saving for rainy days, I welcomed the comparison. But even I knew I could not fully escape the extravagant spending required by my royal station. If some thought my hunting extreme, hers surely was an even worse desperation; a constant race to prove that she was opulently merry and something other than what she'd been born into.

Naturally, the architectural pomp wouldn't strictly be hers, as I donated land for architect Ange-Jacques Gabriel to begin building the Place Louis XV to host the equestrian statue in my honor by Bouchardon, west of the Tuileries garden.

An opportunity to display my forgiving, magnanimous nature came with the Treaty of Aix-la-Chapelle, ending the War of Austrian Succession. While most were displeased with their terms, I was glad to yield our Flemish gains in exchange for peace and letting others have the largest shares. In what I hoped would also be a lesson for Jeanne

Antoinette, a moral zeal filled me to relinquish this greed for more expansion. As if France's glorious name was not already known far and wide! It seemed a small price to pay in exchange for peace and stability for the kingdom.

More importantly, I relished Empress Maria Theresa ceding the duchies of Parma, Piacenza and Guastalla, and setting in motion for my son-in-law Philip to be made Duke of Parma. While giving the Polish throne to Stanislas hadn't succeeded, I could at least try to please my oldest daughter Elisabeth with this new happier position independent of Spain.

Naturally she wanted to visit us at Versailles on the way to her new duchy, and I welcomed the first-born daughter I hadn't seen in ten years as much as did her twin Henriette, and all her joyful siblings. At twenty-one years of age, Elisabeth resembled me as much as her new Gascon accent was foreign and easy to tease. I was just as touched by meeting my seven-year-old granddaughter Isabelle for the first time. I sensed Elisabeth's relief to be away from the oppression of her mother-in-law, Queen Elisabeth Farnese, and her desire to extend her stay before settling down in Parma. There was such laughter and happiness with her and Victoire's returns that I gladly welcomed them to my private *soupers*, and wallowed in the pleasures of family life that I wished didn't feel so temporary.

It was a timely moment for portraits as Nattier delivered those he'd made of our younger daughters in secret. I always remember that time as a rare one when, altogether, we freely shared our emotions. We shed tears at the posthumous portrait of our departed Thérèse in her rosy tones, and took solace in those of Sophie in her gold embroidered gown, and Louise in her pink one, both of whom we hadn't seen in nine years. Recently returned to us, Victoire diffused all the brightness of her fifteen years in her silver grown and gold sash.

Taking advantage of her visit, Elisabeth also sat for Nattier, wearing flowers in her powdered hair and a blue satin cloak, as she handed a lily to her daughter Isabelle at her side, who also posed alone in her cream and gold embroidered gown. Adélaïde also sat for a portrait in a lavender gown, looking every bit the commanding sister with her averted gaze and fan in her hand. But my favorite of all was that of Henriette in her vestal virgin form.

Secretly, discreetly, I acquired two new mistresses, both nobles who were as necessary—and different from Jeanne Antoinette—as they were replaceable. Aside from my natural need, they provided distraction from the mounting population's displeasure at the outcome of the war.

*As stupid as the peace*, they called it, as if their proud opinions were more important than my royal decision! I vacillated between anger and fear at the mounting boldness of these rebellious subjects. Had their trust left me, and how many victories did I need to be kept in their good graces?

An anonymous novel titled *The Indiscreet Jewels* appeared, with myself portrayed as a Sultan with a magic ring that makes women's private jewels speak. When Jeanne Antoinette, who was portrayed favorably, met it with her signature gentle demeanor that refused to utter a bad word, I had the odd impression that she knew the culprit behind it. My soul raged at this unseen yet palpable storm of adversity swelling around me. That she might also be part of tarnishing my image, by trivializing not only my, but even our private relations—and so long as it flattered her, fueled my growing resentment.

I still hadn't fully shaken the incident that had happened a couple of years earlier with my daughter Adélaïde. Her lady-in-waiting, the Comtesse d'Andlau, had given her the famously obscene book *The Story of Dom Bougre*, whose indecent contents on a licentious monk I was reluctant to believe she entirely ignored. That it'd ended up in the hands of Adélaïde with its suggestive illustrations repulsed me as much as it could easily double as an attack on my private affairs. My own natural needs did not mean I wanted my daughters exposed to such filth, and worse, their innocent natures potentially harmed.

Nor could I vocalize the irony that the so-called pleasure this libertine literature meant to praise and inspire were far from anything I'd ever—or would ever even want to—experience. I had the countess put in the Bastille and then exiled, wishing that word of this vile incident hadn't spread to other courts.

Just as disgusting was the newly-circulating libertine novel *Thérèse Philosophe*, that used the Catherine Cadière trial to create a debauched tale of an innocent student and corrupt Jesuit to philosophize on sexual freedom and corrupt religion. An unsettling thought came to me that if Voltaire or his like—and by extension, the willing Jeanne Antoinette—had had something to do with spreading these texts too, it would prove to me yet again that her morals could be as loose in their own way as laid out in these horrid godless tales.

The Dauphin had another stillborn son, fueling his despair at his third dead child. Was it my own sin passed to him, his own, or a combination of both? The one solace was in sharing our sadness together, and at least the Dauphin, after some gentle coaxing from Henriette, had since drawn closer to his second wife Maria Josepha, after the death of his daughter Marie Thérèse, from his first wife.

In my sorrow and anger, I had little patience for marks of defiance. I was kept informed of seditious poetry recitals spreading through Paris, namely one that started by referring to me as a monster with black fury. One person was arrested and sent to the Bastille, until the affair yielded fourteen individuals, in a web that entailed the poem evolving with each person, and created yet others. Worst of all, it was set to song for memorizing and faster spreading. It seemed a continuation of the vile type of song for which I'd recently banished the Comte de Maurepas. Even if I was secretly amused by its reference to Jeanne Antoinette's venereal disease, I couldn't let others so inclined think there wouldn't be consequences.

As base meddlers always seek to benefit from dissatisfaction and chaos, the new title of *Letter on the Blind* was soon tracked down to Diderot, who I relished sending to the Vincennes dungeons. Not only did I disagree with his vain claim that knowledge came from the senses rather than divine revelation, but his removal might discourage others from further grumbling dissent amidst their lingering dissatisfaction over the Treaty of Aix-la-Chapelle.

When not hunting or tending to state affairs, I contemplated my new third and fourth bizarre stag antler acquisitions from Oudry. If anyone should look upon the third painting, they'd likely think of two deformed yet erect phalluses protruding from mangled flesh. It made for a stark example of deformity figuring in nature, while doubling as mischievous nod to my sorry situation with my mistress.

The fourth painting has a majestic long beam with five tines that contrasts its shorter neighbor shaped like a sickle. I liked to think of it as another reflection of life and death facing each other. As I went up and down my private semicircular staircase adorned with this strange expanding collection, I often wondered if I was ascending to my private heaven or deeper into hell. Worst of all, I feared not being able to tell the difference.

Time drifted, as sometimes did my thoughts during Council meetings, as I glimpsed my angora Brillant dozing on his crimson velvet cushion on the mantelpiece... Or his antics of prancing on the table, glad that at least he was enjoying himself. Perhaps it was as the Egyptians said, and this relative to the guardians of the underworld wasn't intimidated by my past experience, when as a twelve-year-old I'd handled Charlotte's new litter with such fervor that three out of the four had died within a day. Just as satisfying was the imposing presence of my pile of antlers on the floor that might magically take life and impale anyone in the room intending me and the kingdom harm.

Before we knew it, Elisabeth finally had to go on to Parma. That bleak mid-October day, my emotional torments were reflected in my children, who struggled to near suffocation with their tears, though the pain had been so harsh for Henriette that she'd fainted several times the previous day. There was no telling when, or if, we'd see Elisabeth again, and though I'd showered her with costly gowns and a trousseau that many at court would frown upon, it still didn't seem enough.

I'd often suspected that I had at least one demon around me, but all doubt was removed in that time. It lurked always, waiting to trap me in the worst way.

With a tone of matter-of-fact indifference, the Beast cited the bad harvests of the two previous '47 and '48 years, filling Paris and surrounding cities with beggars and prowlers of all kinds. What better way to remove these unwanted parasites than to send them to Bicêtre, Salpêtrière, and other General Hospitals for the poor? It'd been done under Louis XIV to address the growing problem of beggary, by gathering them all in one place. At least this time they might not be sent to populate the American colonies, when even children could be of use, especially, in fact, when some preferred them... Not to forget the price per head that would motivate many to fruitful action...

Thunder echoed somewhere and my head pounded as I tried to bring my vision into focus, but all I saw was a shadowy figure with mangled antler-horns, dripping with a foul-smelling muck of tar-like blood. Thick—coating, seeping into the skin, suffocating! How would it ever be wiped off any surface? Vesuvius a mere gentle breeze in comparison!

Did I understand? The Beast asked me, aware of, and relishing my paralyzing confusion. How did it know about me, my weakness—and I suddenly realized that surely more knew about it than I'd ever considered before. Had that been their plan all along? And what had I done to prepare myself? Nothing! Or rather, not enough, despite my momentary spells of piety.

Children? I repeated, my voice grating to keep an even tone lest I show it that pain, too. Better for it to think I was beyond it now, unmoved; maybe even invincible.

Yes; children are so easy to mold to our wishes, and offer a world of new possibilities. That purity is always envied—the Beast stopped, and I heard what it didn't say: that too many take pleasure in corrupting it!

The children would be fooled, seduced, and once trapped, they could be used at will.

But the people recalled the similar gangs of the '20s, so they wouldn't just surrender and submit—I said this flatly, knowing full well that this was a righteous wrath I not only shared with them, but loved them for. Only now did I see why she'd appointed the brutal Chief of Police Berryer, who'd become quickly hated in a short time.

I blinked again and saw before me the dreaded costumed entity I could hardly bear anymore, Jeanne Antoinette in her putrid urine satin gown with maggot-lace and poisonous floral details. With her grotesque rouged cheeks and arrogant manner, I wonder how I'd ever subjected myself and even the Queen and our eldest children to any of her mediocre plays.

What could I say, what could I beg for? That this was a terrible nightmare, a cruel farce I wanted to awaken—or die!—from? How could she, knowing the pain I'd suffered from losing my own children, so nonchalantly suggest to rip others from their own families? And that, with an unshakeable tone that she was better than them, she who'd only reached her highest status because of me! Why was I being punished for giving chances, and not having a harder, violent nature? That I should have to demonstrate more violence to deter it by turns repulsed and allured me.

I saw then that our reaction to evil is sadly not always the glorious one we'd expect and wish of ourselves. At that moment I was not the powerful thirty-nine-year-old king with a loving wife, a brood of children, some victories, and mistresses; I was a frail young boy, trapped, invaded, consumed by others' sickening, defiling greed. At times, often when I thought I'd made progress, the demon resurfaced and ate me up from inside, relishing my desperation that I'd never escape my sin. How could I ever be made clean and whole again?

To whom could I confess that I had no one to turn to: not the Catholic church with its endless shame, guilt, and condemnations, not the Jesuits with their waning influence—in part fueled by the

Beast's hate for them—not the power-hungry Jansenists who, often so similar to the Catholics, possibly outdid even the Catholics in their love of torture and condemnation! The best loving example I'd had was *maman* Ventadour, and she was long gone to her heavenly reward that I could hardly dream of reaching.

As for my enduring manly need, and the Beast's inability to satisfy me, I half listened as she promised to take care of it. She would make sure I am provided with healthy young does of obscure birth who would fulfill their purpose while posing no threat to her position at court. Naturally, it would also limit the risk of ailments and be kept discreet and confidential.

Speechless, I only dumbly nodded. Too late I realized that I'd come to depend on her—and her money for France—too much to protest. Heavy chains locked on me, as I recalled that for years she'd watched me as I hunted, and now I saw that I couldn't escape it except by living it to the bitter end—or ending it in the most sinful way by my own hand.

But as much as I hated her and myself, I would not let her damn myself and my royal inheritance with this worst of cowardly—and criminal!—acts. God knows I'd already harassed Him to know why I lived while He took my children away, so the least I could do was to remain alive until He decided otherwise. She was a mistress of hell, but she was too vain to admit that she would never be the only one.

As I forced my erratic breath to slow, I tried to reassure myself with some of my other delicious secrets that she did not, and would never know about. Only then did I see that my precautions—as wild as they'd seemed—had their own growing basis in reality. For it'd already been a few years since I'd formed my own secret channel of diplomatic measures, whose significant costs I paid for with my own funds.

Meant to advance my own interests when at odds with official French policy, it was known as the King's Secret, begun with my cousin the Prince de Conti as the candidate for the Polish throne.

When the anticipated death of the obese Augustus III didn't manifest, other goals were added to our plans; namely to keep Russia away from European affairs, isolate Austria, and ally with Nordic countries without neglecting Turkey—though with opportunity for these to shift at any moment based on our convenience. That my cousin had his own reasons for hating the low-born Beast henceforth fueled my endeavor to keep going, even as I was also reluctant to give him too much power, and kept him out of the *Conseil.*

Though some aspects of this initiative had its potential benefits of new alliances, it was also a constant reminder that I could never fully trust anyone, and could be betrayed at any moment. Among my best rewards for this tense situation that constantly wavered between security and disaster was the turmoil Jeanne Antoinette displayed at Conti's constant presence, and whose reasons she would never understand, despite all her attempts. Everyone had their secrets and machinations they wanted to apply on me, and I would do the same as necessary.

In light of our new understanding, I changed the Beast's lodgings from Marie Anne's previous quarters to the ground floor, to show her new advisor and prime minister role. She saw fit to commission works of art on the themes of friendship and fidelity, which I found ironic considering La Bruyère's maxims on the very subject. I certainly thought there was truth to his sayings that time, which strengthens friendship, weakens love, and that love and friendship exclude each other.

She commissioned a painting by her favorite portraitist Boucher, showing herself in her silvery-white negligee and rose ribbons, with a pearl bracelet and cameo image of myself at her wrist, as she paused in her sacred *toilette* routine of rouge-application to deign to look at the viewer. What childish artifice! How I wished the mirror would show the delicate masked flower's true misshapen form! If in her many sicknesses—which I dared not name—she was trying to capture and even extend her beauty, it was only another example of her self-serving mastered art of deception that Boucher, in his skill, could soften and dissimulate.

Riots erupted in Paris as children and adolescents aged eight to fifteen disappeared in large numbers in the streets, and furious parents soon traced it to the police. Enraged crowds formed, demanding the return of their children and in the blazing whirl, even lynched a police informant and left his corpse at Berryer's residence, who managed to escape. In this climate of fear, parents grew fearful and preferred to keep their children at home, away from school and the streets.

There was no stopping this storm, even as I suspected what would come. I could not tell them that I understood them, or of my paralyzing helplessness in this situation. I could only hope it would be a temporary measure that would pass over, like so many others, and rightfully blamed on the Beast.

Oh, how I wanted to hold my subjects tight to my bosom, and thank them for their wrath that I fully sanctioned! Considering the rapidity of word-of-mouth, and the enviable loyalty among the lower classes, it was unthinkable for them to doubt my care for them and their struggles. It was evident in my constant difficult decisions, and even the childless Dauphin who'd recently taken a young girl from a poor carpenter's wife he'd spotted in the Versailles gardens. Eager to take care of her, he'd had a genealogy drawn up for her, named her Mademoiselle de Tourneville, and sent her to the convent of Saint-Germain-en-Laye for her education. Or the time that an English noble had dared to call a head clerk a varlet, for which I'd sent him to the Bastille for daring to insult a royal servant! With a plethora of other cases, surely they knew how different we were; that we were not of the same stock as *her*!

If only I could shout at the top of my lungs and expose it all—and maybe then Jeanne Antoinette would finally give up and realize that she'd forgotten what my French subjects, the pulsing heart of the kingdom, were capable of for those they loved! In my frenzy I broke down in grateful tears, as they heard my silent call and delivered her carcass at my feet—knowing it wasn't my fault when I'd been deceived! I prayed for my Queen's sincere lifelong care for the poor to overcome the Beast's mask of benevolence, while filling up these places with children made into slaves for the twisted pleasures of powerful demon-men.

But I was to pay dearly for her filth, when to my great shock, they dared to accuse me and call me Herod! They believed me to be the one calling for this Massacre of the Innocents, bringing about an apocalyptic end—Jansenist or otherwise—that I'd so often yearned for but tried so hard to avoid by peaceful means rather than war! If that wasn't enough, rumors circulated that it was done as part of necessary blood baths for a leprous prince requiring the blood of children or virgins. But my subjects, in their simple love and faith largely unaware of these tales, surely could not think this of me!

The familiar chains tightened at my neck, wrists, and ankles as I realized I would never truly know which of the courtiers played their part in starting, spreading, and twisting such vile rumors with all the others. As the paternal and divinely appointed monarch, I refused to accept that a few mistresses—even some of them sisters—could transform me into a soul-less beast-king marked with Biblical signs of doom.

Unsurprisingly, I had no wish to be near such chaotic barbarity. So in my desire to ride to Compiègne unmolested, I had the ancient *Route des Princes* road upgraded so I could satisfy my rightful urge by avoiding Paris. I would've just liked to see—as per a reliable spy—these puffed up Parisian women reeking of revenge, boasting of marching on Versailles to dethrone me and rip out my eyes, along with killing those responsible members of the police back in Paris! Instead of insulting my position of which they knew nothing but gossip, they should've been grateful that I hunted deer instead of marching to lynch and burn them as they did to countless innocent cats! Let them, and the Beast, think that it was all in her hands, when they knew nothing of my restraint that concealed the power of my secrets that could turn in my favor at any moment!

Meanwhile, the Beast kept at her duty of entertaining me by flinging me from castle to castle, so that I hardly had a moment to think, had I wanted to.

I listened smugly when the Beast relayed the news of a certain Lebeau and his companions chosen by the Parlement as scapegoats to deter further unrest. I held my breath to stifle my trembling, refusing to let on that I didn't want them to die—that I wished to answer the people's call for clemency with that soft-forgiveness I was so often criticized for. But I had to show her and the Parlement that I would not always shrink before defiance, as I so often did with them. I hated myself even more for how it had all come to this. It was easier to ignore the worst horrors when our colonies lay a world away—though I sometimes had nightmares of the accounts of torture and mutilations at Saint-Domingue and elsewhere, as forbidden as it was by the *Code Noir*—but this directly spit in the face of my image and that of benevolent France from my own soil.

How I longed for Pauline Félicité, who should've been there instead and would've never ceased to remind the Beast of her place, no matter how many titles she bought herself or was granted. I was pulled in all directions, and the shattered part of me tried to think that at least these innocent martyrs would temper the bloodthirsty as they departed this evil world that even a king could so rarely control.

The Dauphin became a father again to a daughter named Marie Zéphyrine and, when not hopping from place to place, I passed some time by doing some renovations and furnishing my private chambers in Trianon. I also commissioned Gabriel to design the new French pavilion in the middle of the garden. Based on a vast rotunda, each façade represented a season to delight myself and my special guests away from the court.

But I especially loved its botanical gardens, where time vanished while among our growing collection labeled using Linnaeus's system of plant classification. Amidst the specimens of extracted cell salts from our medicinal plants, pineapple and coffee plants and lavish flowerbeds, I could imagine myself somewhere else while at times alternating between gratitude and envy for not having faced the dangers and gone there myself. To commemorate this development, Jacques-André Portail made a pencil and watercolor including myself and a few others in that charming Trianon gardens scenery.

While the Queen had her music concerts and *cavagnole* games, and the Beast her art and philosophers and their books, I sought refuge in the mysterious mechanical arts and sciences. I'm still struck thinking of the first time I saw the mechanism of the Passemant astronomical clock at Choisy. Designed by watchmakers Passemant and Dauthiau, it displays the time, day of the week, month, year and lunar quarter. For the first time, the official time would be set for the whole kingdom.

More surprising and daring yet, would be the sphere above the clock, where the planets would be seen rotating around the sun. A shiver rocked through me and formed a knot in my core at this strange new creature. Was it blasphemy or timely revelation to have this before me? I appreciated the daring discoveries of learned men, as much as I hoped that the translation of Newton's *Principia* by Fathers Le Seur and Jacquier nearly a decade earlier had helped to ease the Church's ban on the teaching of a heliocentric solar system. If it was discovered that the earth did indeed move around the sun, and not the other way around, wasn't it the Church's task to confirm and inform believers of this knowledge, too? That it had authority in spiritual matters did not make it infallible, when its members were human, and therefore susceptible to mistakes. Though I'd always thought highly of Cardinal Fleury, even I could not call him an infallible man.

As thrilled as I was, it saddened me to think of the Church as being part of stubbornly keeping believers in the dark, and—though I would never say it—just as alarmingly made me wonder what else it could've been wrong about. The clock's mysterious power so allured me that I instantly knew I needed it in my collection.

I also followed the work of the Duc de Chaulnes, Captain-Lieutenant of the Light Horse of the Guard and also astronomer, physician, and Academician who'd already captivated me with his work on the effects of lightning. With his guidance, I commissioned Passemant for one of his new microscopes. Set on a gilded tripod, it pleases me that it is as much a work of science as it is a work of art. My gaze always gravitates to the optical tube decorated in a polished fishskin dyed green. At the top, the ornamental gilt-bronze finial unscrews to reveal an eyepiece on which to correctly position the eye to examine the magnified specimen.

It occurred to me that should the Beast's smashed brains ever be made available for the experiment, I might want to examine them further... But on second thought, there was nothing more I'd want to see or glean from her.

I don't know which would be worse: to say that what I saw in nightmares was the result of copious Champagne and other spirit-drinking and savage eating, or lurking whispering demons manifesting in a way they knew would unsettle and rob me of my final chance to confess...? Running, always running, pursued, watched and judged for all eternity, without hope for rest.

The worst of it was that crushing weight: an animal hide still warm, whose rib cage and massive body stretched over and pressed on me as it first cried like a human child, then snorted out its angry last breaths. The smell—the sickening stench of blood, so thick I was sure I'd throw up all of my own down to the last drop! It was a stag, with one side of its antlers tall with impressive tines, and the other castrated at the base. Its dark eyes blinked, then shifted to bright red, and then it was no longer a stag but a poor, soft lamb; its front and hind legs bound for the slaughter. The blood-soaked creature rose on its feet, breaking off its tying ropes, and as my hands flew up to cover my eyes, in horror I realized antlers protruded in place of my face! *This; THIS is what you're trading me for!* It said, and in that moment I awoke—shaking, sobbing, and hating that I hadn't been swallowed up right then and there for my inescapable guilt.

Unrelenting in their disapproval, my children rallied in wanting the soiled *mother whore* Jeanne Antoinette gone, and it took great self-control to reign in my torrent of explanation. Clearly I would not tell them that the Beast provided and would keep lending the funds the kingdom needed, and that not only had the subduing of the Beast never been as enjoyable as I'd hoped, but it had now come to its physical end. How I wanted to show them that I was on their side, when her inmost stench had always displeased me and only became more bitter and acidic!

I ached to tell them that I fantasized about ending her, but it couldn't be anything as discreet as poison or accident: I'd have to slice her up limb by limb for everyone to see! And I'd be ready, with a great spontaneous speech to finally prove all my deep, refined feelings that salons would talk about for weeks, months; surely even years though it deserved eternity! Would I then become the blameless king—worthy of their enduring love, if I did that which she deserved? No, for even a king has to restrain himself, and worst of all when he shouldn't! So, like me, my children and subjects would have to endure their disappointment, though with the envied benefit of not knowing the full extent of her unscrupulous essence. Yet I never ceased to marvel that perhaps they sensed more through the silence than all the words I could ever say.

In the fall I rode south to Bourron near Fontainebleau to meet my two remaining daughters returning from Fontevraud. With the Dauphin and Victoire as my companions, I tearfully embraced Sophie and Louise whom I hadn't seen in twelve years. As the Queen, the Dauphin and I discovered that their education had once again been wanting, I set my librarian Jacques Hardion to teach them literature, history, some Greek and Italian, and even some philosophy. The twenty-one-year-old Dauphin, with his rigorous education, was also pleased to encourage them and add some Latin, English, astronomy, and geography, along with drawing and music to their overdue repertoire.

What an unutterable joy to see my flock back together, though without the eldest Elisabeth who dwelled in her duchy of Parma. As the eldest at the court, twenty-three-year-old Henriette was most like me in her reserved, yet generous nature endowed with a kind heart. Unsurprisingly, the proud Adélaïde, aged eighteen, took on her self-assigned role of older sister with dutiful enthusiasm, though she soon found that seventeen-year-old Victoire was as gentle as she was independent. We also discovered that sixteen-year old Sophie was shy and self-effacing, while thirteen-year-old Louise had a fire in her piety that diminished the slight hump on her back caused by her curved spine. They collectively fussed over the Dauphin's newborn daughter Marie Zéphyrine, as we all hoped he'd soon be blessed with his own Dauphin. Though I could not hope for the return of my preferred moniker from them ever since the Beast's appearance in our life, I clung to the happy memory of them calling me *Papa-roi*.

I dallied with at least four women that year, among them a young married beauty named Marie Geneviève. The sense of wrong never left me, but like a marionette I felt powerless to overcome my need. Curiously, it also felt increasingly temporary and meaningless, another mask for me to wear for another dreamless or nightmarish night. Perhaps it was my new aim in life: to be so unreachable, and have enough lovers so that most courtiers would not know who had my loyalty at any given moment, just as I couldn't be sure of theirs. I regretted the distance with my own son, as his enduring hate for the Beast, stronger than Henriette and Adélaïde's, along with my delicate situation in it, thwarted our mutual trust.

I commissioned the fifth bizarre stag painting from Oudry, this time featuring a decapitated stag head, with its tongue sticking out to one side and an even set of mid-sized fuzzy antlers, propped up on a wall of stone. The more I looked the more I thought it didn't have to be so shocking or even sad, that its life with such promising signs had been cut short, when even his unshed velvet and mocking tongue had an air of triumphant mischievousness! At least he would live on through the painting, and might even stand out as the one piece in the collection with a full head.

For a time we were soothed, as I became a grandfather again to Elisabeth's son, Ferdinand, born in Parma. In the midst of this, it was not enough for the Beast to spend endlessly, no matter the coffers she had access to while the people demanded bread, or to questionably handle the inconvenient poor and their children. In her endless bourgeoise-elitist wisdom, it was also the moment to reflect our enlightened state by granting support to Diderot for his knowledge reference project with multiple contributors, called *l'Encyclopédie*.

Lest she think I'd been too lenient by shortening his stay at Vincennes to three months, I initially rejected it. It was not that I did not want my peasant subjects to be given due attention for the first time. Nor did I object to them being equally granted access to knowledge to inform themselves and possibly change—or rather, enhance—their thinking. Rather, as Diderot and his kind's past actions had indicated, my reluctance was from the suspected dismissal—or worse, rejection—of the holy word of God, most clearly manifested in their persistent wish to remove the Jesuits from their role in education.

And what would they replace it with instead?

With Pleasure—whatever that meant—and insatiable greed as a convenient cover for other long lists of debaucheries and whose disasters we'd already glimpsed during the Regent? That I had my own struggles of faith and understanding did not mean I wanted their—or anyone else's—version of things. Though I vacillated on granting this to my subjects, I hoped that Diderot's popularity—perhaps in part ironically fueled by his dungeon stint—accurately reflected what my subjects wanted.

As such, as a good father yet again easing his disciplinary grip, I relented, though the irony remained that these volumes would surely not be affordable for the average peasant. What a strange substitute that they might talk and rave about it but not be able to read it for themselves—one might say, fueling another kind of dark ignorance! It seemed yet another opportunity for her—and their—masks, of pretending to want best for others while potentially enriching themselves on others' ignorance. But I could not say this out loud. And in the sweeping wave of eagerness for knowledge, perhaps it might bring in some much needed funds, too, as I naturally monitored its developments. While Benoît XIV's recent *Providas* forbade any Catholic from interacting with Bible-hating Freemasons, I could always call off and censor these publications if necessary. And though I might not always agree with its content, it might help change this idea of me as a despot king who cared only for hunting and mistresses (and when one of these was surely truer than the other). If they had their two-faced strategies, I had mine too.

Putting aside this affair, I rejoiced for the building of the École Militaire to officially begin. Proposed by Maurice de Saxe, and supported by the Beast and the financier Pâris-Duverney, this royal military school would host five hundred impoverished nobles. Not only would it enhance and reflect the education of our regiments, but add to the prestige of my rule through architect Gabriel's impressive work.

My heart soared when, at last, I became grandfather to the Dauphin's son, Louis, the Duc de Bourgogne, ensuring his heir and the continuation of our line. I was so filled with joy that I had little care for expense, and ordered multiple festivities, lowered taxes and—in what would please the Queen—asked the city of Paris to use its substantial funds for festivities as the dowry of poor young girls instead. I did not mind—and in a way, even expected—the silence that the Parisians granted us after the *Te Deum* at Notre Dame, or at l'Hôtel de Ville, as I understood in my own way their mounting anger. The Dauphin and his wife met with the same reception during their own visit, though I hoped he at least somewhat appreciated the insults that were hurled at the Beast, demanding bread and accusing her of killing them.

Another granddaughter, Maria Luisa, was born through Elisabeth in Parma at the end of the year. But soon after, as if ever on time to add to my doubt, I received the news of the passing of the pious Louis, Duc d'Orléans at the Abbey of Saint Geneviève with great shock and sadness. What hope was there for me, or anyone, if this learned, charitable Duc whose deep faith I so envied ended his last days without most of his sanity? Though I doubted the suspicion of him taking Jansenist views, there was irony to him being godfather to my *dévot* Catholic Dauphin. Sadly, the suspicion of Jansenism had been enough for him to be refused communion, though thankfully he received the last rites from his own chaplain. I also thought of his protégé Marie-Angélique, who'd surely lose her place at the convent and have to seek lodging elsewhere.

Then, another stab to my heart came with the death of my Henriette from smallpox, just a few days later. We were all shocked at the rapidity of her decline, and I wondered if I'd been selfish to ask her to accompany me on a sledge ride a few days before. Was it the natural cold or my own that had killed her? Before I could decide it would've saved her life not to come, I told myself I was no one to tell God to change His plans. But only twenty-four! It was too short and yet more than I deserved at the same time. I spent the next day alone, hunting in a daze, without uttering a word or really looking at anything. The next day the Dauphin and Mesdames attended the ceremony to give holy water, except for Adélaïde who was too wracked by grief. Her remains were buried at Saint-Denis, while her heart was interred at the Abbey of Val-de-Grâce, founded and beloved by Anne of Austria in gratitude for her pregnancy with Louis XIV.

Drained, I retreated to Trianon alone for weeks, though in the mornings I dutifully went to the château to meet for councils or with ministers. I tried to think that at least she'd seen me ban l'*Encyclopédie*, whose two volumes in less than a year had increasingly infuriated *dévots* like herself and her siblings, along with the Jesuits, the King's Council, and Jansenists, among others. Something told me that even if I should not succeed in preventing its printing and circulation, I'd at least done my part in showing my rejection and done what I could to stop it.

The next month our sadness was added to with the Dauphin's still-born daughter. His third among five pregnancies, it made us cherish his daughter Marie Zéphyrine and son Louis Joseph all the more. As I'd come to know, pain could have a way of bringing some closer together, and I welcomed that with my own daughters, whose silly nicknames I gave them granted some much-needed lightness. We talked of Henriette, and of the lovely painting she'd recently had of Nattier where she represented the element of fire, while her twin Elisabeth had posed as earth, Adélaïde as air, and Victoire as water. In honor of her memory and love of music, I decided to have Nattier paint Henriette in a red brocade dress embroidered with gold thread, and her beloved viola da gamba.

I tried not to take it personal when twenty-year-old Adélaïde was caught in the spring having gifted a snuffbox along with an anony-mous note to one of my young guards. That she, as my oldest daughter at court, would think of such things—and with such an undeserving subject!—so soon after her sister's passing made me angrier at her than I'd ever been. I resolved to keep a close eye on her and sent him to the edge of the kingdom with a pension to keep him away.

I had to marvel that we might be strangely passing each other our inner torments when in the summer the Dauphin fell sick with small-pox, but thankfully recovered.

I whisked away to Fontainbleau and passed some time with Char-lotte Rosalie, and I knew that I hadn't lost all my sensation when my main satisfaction was in her entourage's secret attempt to have her replace the Beast. But there were moments when even that, and everything else, became so meaningless that I only wanted to go where Henriette had gone to watch over my other children, and grandchil-dren.

Elisabeth sent aching words of longing too, as much for her missing twin as for her happier years at Versailles, and expressed her wish to die in France and to rest with her twin in due time. That had to be why Henriette had been hysterical at their last goodbye; filled with their mysterious twin-bond sense that whispered it would be the last time they'd see each other on this earth...

As usual we welcomed Elisabeth's visit, and in the months of new births, torment, overwhelm and emptiness, my children's interactions with Jeanne Antoinette eased, which, if nothing else, gave some variety. With all my daughters home and Adélaïde not bearing to stay in the apartments where Henriette had died, I began renovations to have her and Victoire move closer to me. That it displeased jealous Jeanne Antoinette was all the more reason to get it completed as soon as possible.

With her increasingly common bouts of coughing, fevers, chest pains and breathlessness that led her to use the flying chair, I had added reason—and amusement—to keep away from her newest charade of imitating the pious Madame de Maintenon. After all, she could be contagious—until I tried to remind myself that I'd already been inoculated by years of suffering and sickness, and that, since it hadn't happened yet, my own health was proof that I would not fall by her hand.

What's more, she flattered herself in providing me with younger, unknown virgin girls at the discreet Parc-aux-Cerfs, to provide for my needs without having to worry about disease, or introducing these temporary interests to court. At first I thought I would simply visit these girls and leave them chastely untouched, for Jeanne Antoinette and her entourage to realize that her suggestions were not to my liking.

Was I a dog to simply eat whatever she put on my plate? As willing as they were, I doubted these girls would know anything about pleasing me, when my bouts of numbness to anything life had left to give only seemed to increase. What irony, that I could be the one to teach them some things, when I'd never thought of, nor wanted to see myself as such.

But in this simple place, devoid of suffocating Versailles etiquette, I glimpsed an air of innocence that made me long for this purity I'd often felt barred from. It surprised me to think that in some ways, I might not be so different from these girls, and that they might even have more power over me than I did over them, even with my real royal identity concealed. What if I could regain some of my own lost innocence by sharing it with an untouched beauty who wanted to share this moment of intimacy, and maybe even one of brief security for us both? That I might for once be the one to offer security when I still longed for the maternal kind at once humbled and inspired me.

If they were in shy awe of me as the first man before them, so was I with them, and I knew I could not go further unless we prayed together before the act. Though I hoped my handsomeness would help to please, I did not want to hurt them, and if they remembered nothing else pleasant from me, at least we'd taken a moment to remember our shared Creator.

Just as importantly, it pleased me thoroughly for Jeanne Antoinette to notice that I still dallied with other ladies of the court, lest she think herself once again safe from threat. Her constant torment on that account was only fitting punishment for all the suffering she'd already caused. In constant proof of her audacity—masked by her longing for my friendship, that most stupid word for a mistress!—she dared to suggest merging my royal line with hers by marrying her daughter Alexandrine to Charles, the son given to me by Pauline Félicité. The wicked witch! I would never do such a thing, and if only she'd lived surely none of this would've happened to begin with! What arrogance; to think I would soil her precious memory and ancient royal line by mixing it with that of a mere conniving bourgeoise, no matter how much money she had!

Her failure on that count no doubt further inspired her next blow that I'd suspected would come next, namely her demand to dismiss Charlotte Rosalie, the first of her real competitors. The Duc de Choiseul, related to Charlotte's husband, had uncovered the plot of Charlotte replacing Jeanne Antoinette, and as her protégé, the Duc de Choiseul naturally warned her about it. That made little difference to me either way, so I went along with that and even elevated Jeanne

Antoinette to Duchess, to go along with the prime minister duties of state and international affairs she liked to fanatically manage. All the better if her Jezebel-inspired obsession for power consumed her sooner than she, and any of us, expected. I would remind it as often as needed: that I was at the top of the Great Chain, and if anything, seeing them all shaking like leaves as they tried to decipher and maneuver my real, committed interests and undertakings was a balm to my soul.

As another distraction and reward, I commissioned my sixth bizarre stag antler painting from Oudry. I couldn't say which was my favorite, and in the ever pleasant-bitter melancholy they brought me, I resolved that it would be the last from this personal collection whose first image would forever be tied to the memory of Pauline Félicité's pregnancy and gruesome death.

Eager—and deserving!—to escape in my temporary world of elusive pleasure, I welcomed the distraction of my valet Lebel tracking down a young beauty named Marie-Louise O'Murphy. I'd first heard about her from Jeanne Antoinette's brother, Abel-François, who'd showed me the erotic backside portrait of her by Nattier that she'd supposedly posed for.

While duplicates of the portrait were fast being made and acquired by yearning men, I naturally had the priority in setting her aside for myself. For the first time, I was moved to see how a young beautiful girl, from such an unfortunate criminal family of prostitutes and thieves, could still be miraculously untainted by their doings. I fell under the spell of her glowing Irish youth, wrapped in her Catholic superstitions that added to our child-like burgeoning love. After comfortable housing at the Parc-aux-Cerfs, I had a new charming house made for her where I could visit her at leisure. Soon I couldn't spare her presence, and Lebel made arrangements as I brought her with me to Compiègne, la Muette, and Crécy. I'd added at least six other mistresses to my list that year, but I instantly knew that la Belle Morphise, as I liked to call her, would be my delightful favorite and priority for some time.

In the meantime the court found amusement in the ongoing Quarrel of the Bouffons that argued over the musical merits of the French versus the Italian opera. Naturally, the lovers of French opera in the tradition of Lully—via Rameau—were in the King's corner, while those of Italian opera in the tradition of Pergolesi were in the Queen's corner. Siding with the Italian opera, Rousseau presented us *The Village Soothsayer* at Fontainebleau, with the male character of Colin played by Jeanne Antoinette, though rightfully in a skirt rather than breeches. I thoroughly enjoyed its premise of two lovers suspecting each other of unfaithfulness who seek the advice of the soothsayer and, after a series of deceptions, reconcile and marry. I even went so far as to offer Rousseau a life pension for it, though when he refused the great honor I was as much relieved as I was concerned he was avoiding any sense of loyalty to me.

Much more scandalous was the reaction to Voltaire's satirical poem *The Maid of Orléans*. Not only was it a licentious mockery of the medieval Jeanne the Maid that lampooned superstition, it also denigrated Jean Chaplain's own heroic poem *La Pucelle* from the previous century. In case he and Jeanne Antoinette needed further reminding, it was promptly censored and added to the National Library's list of texts forbidden to the public.

As gossip spread about my precious Belle Morphise, I showered her with all the care and affection I could as we awaited the full term of her pregnancy. To our mutual sadness she had a miscarriage, and that it nearly cost her her life only endeared her to me in her unwavering love and loyalty in my service. While the Queen had certainly given me ten children, Morphise did not distance herself or shut her door to me despite the danger. Nearly convinced that she could do me no wrong, I would let nothing disrupt my complete, consuming obsession with her.

In its own way, it also fueled my own affection for the Queen. After years of her painting hobby and renditions that she made for herself, her friends, and father, the Queen's artistic talent yielded a successful copy of Oudry's bucolic *Farm*. Originally made as per the Dauphin's precise instructions, it represented his vision of an ideal France with man in harmony with nature. I smiled at its innocence and luminous colors that so differed from the previous darker depictions of dead game and hunts. Amidst the gentle activities of farm life, I noticed the dog who'd caught a duck as the others escaped, while various animals reclined around the pond. Though Oudry preferred to paint from real-life, I appreciated this scene from my son's own mysterious imagination that the Queen had in turn recreated for me. If she wasn't so self-deprecating I would've said to her, without fear of mutual embarrassment, that her talent yielded a faithful rendition that was as pleasant as any seen at the Salon. Instead, I received her gift with pleasure.

We rejoiced at the birth of the Dauphin's second son, Xavier, Duc d'Aquitaine, while at the Salon Nattier displayed the lovely portrait of his daughter Marie Zéphyrine wearing a cream embroidered gown and playing with a dog. Nearby was the portrait of Marie Geneviève Boudrey as a Muse in the act of drawing. Though an undeniable beauty, it was already a bygone fling that I did not miss given my happiness with la Belle Morphise, and the two new brothers since given to Marie Zéphyrine.

A different feeling of power seized me when I welcomed the Passemant clock to its designated Clock Room at Versailles. At last, after nearly thirty years in its making, I had the glorious human-like gilded bronze cabinet by Caffieri that houses the precious mechanism by Passemant and Dauthiau available for my instant access. It stands at over six feet tall on four legs, with its head-like crystal planisphere where the planets rotate around the sun. Under it is the clock at chest level, then a calendar at torso level, and the pendulum between the legs at bottom. With the glass backing and added mirror, I could glimpse at its mechanism at the rear, and marvel at its ability to reach the year 9999. The more I looked at it, the more secrets and possibilities it revealed, exchanging my sense of time for another kind. I resolved to make a new tradition of watching it delightfully change at every New Year's Eve.

I welcomed yet other delightful time-keepers in the form of miniature watches, made by a talented young clockmaker named Caron. His recent feud with his previous mentor, the famed royal watchmaker Lepaute, who'd stolen his inventive idea and published it in the *Mercure de France* as his own, had thankfully garnered Caron the attention he deserved. I requested his presence at court to present his new invention, and claiming to be able to make a watch as small as a ring, I set him on to the task for Jeanne Antoinette. When he delighted us with his marvelous delivery, I gladly removed Lepaute's title of royal matchmaker and made Caron Purveyor to the King. While Jeanne Antoinette might've loved her gift as another token of her talent for merging the sciences and fashion, I appreciated it as a symbol that the object would outlive her own limited time.

Less than six months after his birth, my grandson Xavier, Duc d'Aquitaine joined his three dead siblings. I cried like a baby, wishing that the Dauphin and I didn't have in common the loss of four children. Fearing again that my son was being punished for my sins, I pleaded to God that at least they might be reunited in the beyond under the gentle care of Henriette.

As the weight of unpredictable, changing time pressed on me, more renovations were in order. I removed the Seashell Room in favor for the King's Staircase, and replaced the Oval Room with a discreet private chamber and water closet, with angular walls and wooden panels, located just behind my inner office. It was to be a precious, much-needed secluded Dispatch Room for my most secret state affairs, so I might as well do it surrounded by books and pastoral scenes by Domenchin de Chavanne and Boucher's teacher, Galloche.

Life in, life out—such is God's eternal cycle. A summer blow came, and for once it was one that was only fitting. Jeanne Antoinette's daughter Alexandrine fell sick at the Paris convent she'd been placed in, and by the time the two doctors I sent arrived, she'd already died.

I had nothing against the girl, and even envied her ability to strike so deep at her core. Fly, fly far away from here—and from *her*! I wanted to scream.

Her mother and I had both known what it was like to lose a child, and though I did not see my illegitimate ones, I knew of their whereabouts and provided for them, with money and titles to ensure them a better life. I did not rip them—or other children—from their families to be handed to depraved demons who debauchedly preyed on their innocence, then discarded to live in horrid conditions at some dilapidated poorhouse.

Oh—if I thought of it too long I'd finally go and seek out a weapon that would annihilate them all. But in all my vanity I knew I couldn't be entirely lost when I still stopped and asked myself: was I God to do so? I knew the Beast would, and that's why she would not have my sympathy, but only my strengthened gratitude that God's will would always have its way. Though she hardly deserved it, she could try to console herself with her brother Abel-François's role in having the artists Cochin and Bellicard along on his travels, and whose recently published drawings on Herculaneum became an immediate sensation.

I had further reason to discard any sadness, when a few days later la Belle Morphise gave birth again, this time to a healthy baby girl, Agathe Louise. I had her immediately put into the care of a wet nurse, and resolved to later have her educated in a convent and appointed two trustworthy men as her legal guardians. Though I'd always pride myself that most could not read my emotions, Jeanne Antoinette surely sensed that joy, too. Even the Quarrel of the Bouffons, once a playful rivalry between French and Italian opera, had since become bitterly politicized, with her *Encyclopédistes* supporters siding with the Italian, while the nobles and other *Encyclopédistes* opponents defended the French opera tradition.

The sense of mounting carnage robbed me of rest, as insatiable anxiety ate me up in light of our relentless, and most dangerous,

English enemy. Mayhem erupted at the American colonies when a young Major Washington appeared at our Fort LeBoeuf, relaying the outrageous claim that it was English territory and that the French had to leave! As if we would just surrender the entire Ohio River Valley and let them have it all! The valley—crucial to trade transport and the heart of the continent—was too important for our empire that stretched from New France in the north to Louisiana, along the Mississippi River. Surely we could not let the English simply take over and have full dominion of the continent.

But they seemed unscrupulous enemies bent on any barbarity when Washington's surprise attack resulted in Frenchmen savagely scalped and killed—with the help of his Iroquois allies—and the assassination of our French Canadian military officer, Jumonville. I shuddered to think of Jumonville taken as a prisoner of war, then struck dead by the Iroquois Tanacharison's tomahawk to his head, in the midst of conversation with Washington.

What was I supposed to think? Was Washington truly ignorant of this intent, when he'd signed a document admitting that he'd been assassinated? I didn't know which was the preferred scenario: that the English had once again possibly stirred trouble resulting in this illegal murder of a diplomatic envoy, or that Tanacharison had his own reasons for resorting to this barbarity.

I recalled the Natchez revolt and our attempt to drive them off that had sparked the Chickasaw Wars, with whom they'd lived. Though the Natchez had soon ceased to be a threat, I dreaded that our failure to overcome the Chickasaw, allied to the English, was now proving to their advantage against us and our Indian allies. Gloom filled me as I hoped the Indian embassy who'd visited us nearly thirty years before still thought as fondly of me as I did of them, even as they might suffer for their loyalty to us. Alarmingly, peaceful resolution with Britain seemed increasingly unlikely.

Having lost Xavier but a few months earlier, we welcomed the news of the birth of the Dauphin's third living son, Louis, Duc de

Berry. I pondered what the future might hold for my son, and my two grandsons, and had the strange idea that the world they'll live in might be nearly unrecognizable. Reluctantly it occurred to me that the Dauphin, with his unwavering strong sense of morality, might one day be a better ruler than I, though I suspected his sheltered idealism might also suffer some blows. For all of his love of the Catholic Church, he knew as well as I the mounting strain to our French Gallican tradition seeking autonomy from Rome. I wished I could hand him an indesctructible French Catholic church that set Rome and the angry Jansenists firmly in place, even as I grew increasingly doubtful of it.

How many wars could one fight at once? For I increasingly dreaded my deadlock before so much opposition on all fronts. With the War of Austrian Succession leaving us nearly bankrupt, Jeanne Antoinette had played her part in creating the *vingtième* tax, the first ever to be applied to the privileged nobles and the church, though I knew the clergy might have ways of exempting themselves. Unsurprisingly, it was soon contested, along with the resurgence of protest over the Bull *Unigenitus* that condemned Jansenism.

All of a sudden, this bull that had been made state law by Cardinal Fleury seemed on the verge of tearing the kingdom apart, led by the angry Parlement-supported Jansenists. The latest spark had been the *billets de confession*, papers affirming submission to the bull that suspected Jansenists had to sign, or risk being refused the last sacraments and burial in consecrated ground. As such, this feud between the Roman Catholic Church deemed as interfering in the French church, brought the civil justice system to a halt.

In response to this lawless defiance and divisions, I reminded them that I was the Absolute master once more, and exiled the Parlement. With nearly everyone's hate on my shoulders shrinking my already small circle of trusted support to lean upon, after some time I resolved once again to reinstate it as a peaceful gesture—and so long as they kept silent on *Unigenitus*. After sixteen months of exile they returned, and they lost little time in defying me yet again, seeking and finding self-serving nomenclature to counter my royal order of silence. Had Cardinal Fleury been wrong? And worse, I a weak king whose authority no longer deserved to be heeded? I had the paralyzing impression of an irreparable wrong that I could not overcome. I surrendered, though wearing boots and hunting attire to express my displeasure, feeling like my grasp was weakening and my madness deepening by the moment.

While seeing la Belle Morphise at times helped to ease my nerves, I relished most my time with the Prince de Conti—who'd also been part of maneuvering the Parlement debacle—made of sumptuous dinners and secret affairs. I loved the camaraderie between us; due in his part to his blatant dislike for Jeanne Antoinette, while part of my amusement was in my own secret stance. Her pathetically increasing obsession over deciphering the nature of our affairs was another reason to bring us close together in our mutual goal of keeping her away. If she thought that putting on her saintly air from her mounting health concerns and the recent death of Alexandrine would be enough to undo all the harm she'd caused, she had a lot more to learn. Her secret negotiations with Jesuits—whom she hated—to stabilize her position were no secret to me. Amidst my disgust that she'd done much to fuel, I was nearly certain that if I ever forgave her, it would be a long time yet.

Then it was time to bid adieu to Jean-Baptiste Oudry, the beloved painter who'd created hunting pieces for me for nearly thirty years. I swallowed my emotion at the impressive panoramic portrait he'd made of my twenty-year-old self and my entourage hunting at Saint-Germain. Just as precious to me were my six bizarre stag antler pieces, the first of which had captured viewers at the Salon in the midst of my mourning for Pauline Félicité. I vowed to treasure the work he'd left us, just as he'd turned down offers by Tsar Peter the Great and the King of Denmark in his loyalty to remaining in France.

Another shock came with the death of five-year-old Marie Zéphyrine, who couldn't officially be mourned given her age. As was becoming familiar, I lost my rigorous appetite, and redoubled my prayers, trying once more to drown my sorrow by merging memories of our children to the tune of Vivaldi's soothing "Spring." I hoped it could be accepted as a humble offering to my son's worthy prayers, who now buried his fifth child among seven, as the eighth was set on joining us shortly.

Had the end of the world come upon us? There was little else we could think as we pondered the brutal Lisbon earthquake. On this beautiful morning of All Saint's Day, the catastrophe struck Europe's most Catholic kingdom early in the morning. The sky darkened with dust and debris, burying thousands as others fled to the docks for safety, only to find that the Tagus River had receded enough to reveal shipwrecks. Monstrous tsunami waves followed, causing damage as far as Scotland, and even the coasts of Brazil whose gold had so benefited the Portuguese. Fires erupted, with vicious winds that caused suffocation and spread ravenously, as if competing with the earthquake itself for the most carnage.

The question that weighed on all the survivors—and the whole of Europe—was the source of its cause. Catholics thought it a punishment for the presence of freethinkers and atheists, while Protestants saw it as retribution for the Catholic Portuguese inquisition. Were we next, with all our religious and economic upheaval? Even the Passemant clock had stopped when its tremors reached us! My chest tightened to think it ever happening to our kingdom—and when it'd been felt as far as Finland—while the familiar dread and fascination warred in me. God was all-powerful, and yet, perhaps some scientists were right in thinking that it also had some other, more natural explanation.

What if both views did not have to exclude one another, but each used their own language to explain it? If the most Catholic kingdom had been unable to avoid it—there'd been no signs, after all—then it seemed vain to think anyone else could. And yet, that there might be things we could learn about it granted a hint of unexpected reassurance. Still, it did nothing to stifle my fear of what France might suffer because of me. Annoyingly, I suspected that it was only a matter of time before Voltaire had something less than uplifting to say about it.

About a week later, watchmaker Caron was introduced at court. He mentioned sitting for his portrait by Nattier, and I was pleased to know his client list would grow from his talent of making time appear as beautiful and intriguing as it could be terrifying.

Yet another week later, the Dauphin welcomed his fourth living son, Louis Stanislas, Comte de Provence, who joined his four-year-old, and one-year-old older brothers. With my three grandsons outnumbering the legitimate sons I'd had, I tried to take it as a good omen for the future of France. It also pleased me to think that Marie-Angélique, the wild girl who'd been among us for nearly twenty-five years, might inspire sympathy with the new account written on her life by Mme. Hecquet.

It was easy to wonder about signs and be certain sure we'd follow a better course if only we had them. And yet I—in my pride, in my twisted love, in my indifference—hadn't managed to think far enough with the Beast. For once, I thought my numbness a sound defense when on that late November day she jealously lashed out at me about Morphise, demanding her immediate removal. What if the Queen died and I married Morphise, leaving the Beast cast aside, mocked, and isolated after everything she'd done? Had I forgotten all the secrets she'd been part of, and could supply the pamphleteers with even more material to hasten my own end? Cornered like a stag, I saw that what I'd feared for so long, but had half-thought a figment of my wild imagination had finally happened: not only was she blackmailing me, but perhaps it'd been her plan all along in securing herself control.

Should I have been oddly touched by this desperate Beast who'd conveniently discarded—and then in turn been rejected by her husband when trying to reconcile with him? And who, given my distance and her own frail health, had little left to live for with her daughter also gone?

No.

Even if I hadn't considered marrying Morphise, even had the Queen been ill, I would not appease her with that information.

Every bone in my body wanted to contest her demands—maybe even end her right there and then! But even that she'd use as another way to turn my caring protective power against me by making herself a victim. Though I would suffer no matter the course, my triumph remained in that she would not dictate my affection despite the circumstances.

So in my feigned indifference that was more grace than she deserved, I agreed to repudiate Morphise and let her do as she wanted for my next arrangements. At four in the morning, Morphise was ordered to leave and hastily married off to a well-born, appealing young man. I contented myself that the woman the Beast had chosen to replace her was none other than Morphise's plain older sister Brigitte. As different as they were, I could at least share my affection for her sister with her.

As if reading my mind, the Prince de Conti soon had another idea. Perhaps even more eager than myself to supplant the Beast, he presented to me another mistress, the Marquise de Coislin, and that she was from the House of Mailly and his idea was all that I needed. What was another dalliance when this might finally rid us of the Beast? Among all the forgotten names, it could end up being one of the few of greatest importance! But the Beast would not take this threat to her rule, and soon kept the Marquise at such a distance from me that she left court.

As guilty consciences are often plagued by paranoia, I did not share the Beast's mounting concern that he was conspiring against us. Rather, I saw his rumored attempt to incite the Huguenots to rebellion as his display of power against her. He was hardly the religious kind, and regardless, it wasn't his fault if he was the descendant of two major participants in the previous century's Fronde civil wars.

Another mask was revealed when Frederick II, who'd previously been our ally during the War of Austrian Succession, insultingly deserted me by signing the Anglo-Prussian Alliance, allowing Britain to focus on pillaging our colonies. In response to this reversal of alliances, I signed the Treaty of Versailles with Austria, offering mutual assistance if attacked by Britain or Prussia. Soon after, the English declared war on France, and I struggled to brace myself as the lingering dissatisfactions from the terms of the Treaty of Aix-la-Chapelle resurfaced, with long arms once more bent on reaching everywhere for their own shares. I had the raging-intoxicating thought of invading Britain and claiming it as ours, as they'd first dared to do at our Fort Le Boeuf across the Atlantic. I had sought to avoid conflict for so long, but if the boiling world wanted it, perhaps this Diplomatic Revolution was what we needed to set things straight.

As the war broke out, the Prince de Conti wished for commandment of the armies of the Rhine to assist Empress Maria Theresa, but I refused as the Beast preferred naming the Prince de Soubise instead. It was hardly surprising when, though I hardly liked to consider it, I was not deaf to her enduring suspicions about my cousin. But with our bond and history of secret diplomacy, I'd make no such assumptions until I was sure.

In the meantime, the Prince de Conti was still the assumed head of the decade-old *Secret du Roi*, to which I'd added a new member who was one of his acquaintances. Hailing from a poor noble family from the Tonnerre region of Burgundy, Charles-Geneviève d'Éon de Beaumont was a contributor to Fréron's *Année littéraire*, a publication that countered the influence of the *Encyclopédistes* philosophers. He'd also garnered attention with his political writings through two works on finance and administration. With the recent rapprochement of the English and Prussian dynasties, I wanted a bold triple alliance of France, Austria, and Russia. There was something about this young man, rider since the age of six—whose first two names combined my son with Pauline Félicité and Paris's female patron saint—and his confidence that made him perfect for the task. As such, I sent Charles-Geneviève to the Russian court to begin the exchange, though with express request not to whisper a word of it to Conti.

Hidden in a copy of Montesquieu's *L'Esprit des Lois*, I sent the letter to Empress Elizabeth suggesting we undertake a confidential diplomatic exchange. It had to be the thrill of the secret chase that even had me playfully considering adding another *galant* letter, reminding—or perhaps informing—her how close she'd come to being my spouse despite the snubbing that I had no part in.

In it, I'd confess how I'd thought of her the first time I was intimate with the Queen and that, as the daughter of Tsar Peter whom I thought of fondly, she'd surely be as enthusiastic in private as she was gracious in public. Better yet, she might read my mind without my having to ask: how did it feel to rule with terror that no one dared defy her? How long was the sense of quiet peace that followed the whipping or cutting of tongues? How often I'd wished I could do the same! But as always, something told me that even that wouldn't stop their poisonous slander from spreading!

Then I'd add that, if she should ever do like her father and visit, she might join me on the hunt. Or we might enjoy strolling the gardens as we discussed her abolishment of capital punishment and her Russian Orthodox faith, which her father had been willing for her to change to marry me... Or perhaps even why she was unmarried and childless. I imagined that in some ways it was freer, and less painful that way. But like so much else, it was just another fantasy to relish and keep to myself.

Jeanne Antoinette—after my negotiations with the Queen to eradicate some of her gambling debt—became lady-in-waiting to the Queen, granting her the most noble rank possible for a woman at court. To announce that achievement, she sat for Boucher in her green silk gown, looking as self-satisfied as her so-called learned *Encyclopédistes* philosopher friends represented by the book in her hand.

She moved the porcelain factory from Vincennes to Sèvres, near her Bellevue estate. In my bouts of shaken confidence, I could at least boast that our prized porcelain had become renown throughout Europe, and even surpassed that of Meissen.

The Dauphin had another stillborn son, keeping his number to three.

Then, the dreaded moment came; that of shedding the mask I'd so willingly excused. With my cousin's continued efforts to incite Protestants against me—when we were fighting against two such powers, while his enemy Jeanne Antoinette pushed for a 'Catholic' alliance with Austria—I felt once again on the brink of incurable madness. How had it come to this? In his anger over repeated disappointments and slights, including from *her*, it tore me to think he might've joined the growing fanatical factions in rejecting my divine royal position.

I could understand his wishful thought that it might finally grant him the evasive power he yearned for. But as much as he'd wanted a crown, and failed to earn the Polish one through our secret diplomacies via the *Secret du Roi*, was he truly set on irreparable sedition and treason? How could he, when I'd recently tried to help him with a huge sum to pay off his considerable debts! Or was I the foolish one for shrugging off his past questionable morals, when he'd scandalously enriched himself during Law's System that severely depleted the Royal bank?

His jealousy and anger must've blinded him into thinking I'd have Jeanne Antoinette ruling instead of him, when the truth was they would each remain in their limited positions as I saw fit. While I'd never say it aloud that I'd often envied his charisma that seemed to earn him endless friends—now chief among them the Parlement who opposed me—he was only proving to me that even that wouldn't suffice.

How like the Beast he seemed, when in his own growing pompous power—always so certain they could do better than me, when I'd contributed to their fortune!—he raged in perpetual discontent. What irony that they should want to have my power—or another version of it—when they'd still have to contend with each other in my absence! With all of this, losing this confidant so shook me that I nearly begged him not to desert me. But I knew all too well that I'd have to carry on either way, as it increasingly seemed everyone left me sooner rather than later. Meanwhile, I shifted such communication to Jean Pierre

Tercier, who increasingly seemed the candidate to take over his position.

Then came January 5th, 1757.

How many times did I have to face death before finally leaving this place? It seemed nearly once every decade: 1712, 1721, 1744—1757.

I still wonder if a part of me would've been happier that morning had I known what was coming. Perhaps I would've let the blade go deeper, maybe even thanked him.

I was entering my carriage when Robert-François Damien was bold enough to evade my guards and plant his penknife into my chest. As the Dauphin yelled and commotion spread, I realized that though my thick winter clothing had protected me, the blood on my hand announced the end had come, and so I called for my confessor.

The Queen, Mesdames and the Dauphine rushed over from Trianon in a panic, and with a croaking voice, I asked the Queen and my daughters to forgive my wrongs and scandals. To the twenty-seven-year-old Dauphin I said that his rule had come, that the kingdom was in good hands, and I hoped he'd be happier than I'd been—thus unleashing our torrential tears.

Fearing that my sinful soul would be whisked away to hell at any moment, I demanded a second confession, and eventually even had a third. Time stood still as so many faces fixed on me, silent and yet full of dreadful things neither of us wanted to say. The Beast wasn't there—I'd never call her to join the side of my family—and yet she was, when the opposition she brought fueled unrest in my kingdom. Like so many others, she'd hardly even truly care about my fate, but only feign it as she contested being sent away like Marie Anne.

They took Damien away to be tortured and to uncover his collaborators, which revealed nothing. He was found with a Jansenist book of prayers, whose author Pasquier Quesnel had so vehemently stirred Louis XIV to condemn him in the Bull *Unigenitus*. But that in itself couldn't answer everything, and just as senseless; what if Damien had carried it on purpose to throw us off? With all the fanatical conspiring,

I didn't know which was worse: that it could once more be the work of an English spy, or that someone closer to the court could've had a hand in it, too.

Though two days later I was out of physical danger, it was only to make clearer the wounds to my heart and soul. Whether it was the act of several or one, here was the worst proof that I was hated enough to inspire regicide—the first time since Ravaillac assassinated Henri IV in 1610.

But no matter their fickle emotions and anger, they knew as well as I that I was still the sacred king endowed with a sacred body designated to rule over them in that time. I'd been defied in the worst way, and yet I'd survived even this vile attempt! Surely they would pray for me again as they had at Metz, and it would not be repeated; maybe it'd even make me look still beloved by God, a bit more invincible... Though people were evil, God had his mysterious ways.

Morbid days turned into nights, and in my hazy nightmares I saw the Beast grimacing and pressing down on her ears as thousands of children surrounded her, screaming: *guilty, guilty, guilty*! And then I joined in with them, too, incessantly crying but also curiously enjoying every second.

Eight days later she was before me: nodding her horned head that reassured me that there was no conspiracy; he was a madman who'd get his punishment. Her snake-tongue added that there were rumors that his daughter had been kidnapped during the Paris riots seven years before, but even if that were true, she'd been returned to him, as others had. And now his daughter sat in the Bastille with his wife and father, deserving of banishment. *Unlucky girl: if only her mad father had let it go! These kinds of people just don't know better!*—sighed the Beast.

Even in my frail state, I did not let on that amidst her Devil speech I regained my strength. Just as I thought, it was not my fault when she'd had her dirty hand in it. And though once more my life had been threatened, she—and everyone else!—now saw that they would never succeed in toppling me. Her ways might come back to haunt me at any moment, but she and her minions would not win. They called Damien crazy, and all kinds of names—as they did me—and though we weren't, we both owed parts of that to her, too.

I wanted to scream and make her see how evil she was for shrugging off his pain, as if it could just be washed away...! Until I remembered I shouldn't have to do that. By turns I trembled and seethed to imagine the extent of what he knew, and worse, thought me the source! Though my mounting rage seemed to have no end, I could not let it consume me. In my self-doubting awareness of my limits and wish to try something else, too late I saw that I should've never let this Jezebel into men's political affairs.

Once more, this case and trial was in the hands of the Parlement, who never succeeded in getting him to confess to any accomplice or much about his motives. The most I could gather was that he'd been repulsed by the Archbishop of Paris Christophe de Beaumont's refusal to give sacraments through his *billets de confession*, and something along the lines that none of it would've happened if it hadn't been for that.

I couldn't help but marvel at this defiant creature. Did Damien really care about this doctrinal measure, or had he chosen it, instead of exposing the lasting effects of pain his daughter had suffered? Though he seemed to be alone in his act, it seemed like everyone had their own hand in it, whether intentional or not. The Jesuits who favored papal supremacy over me, the Jansenists, the Protestants, the Jews, the freethinkers, the peasants, the nobles, the court, down to my closest who'd claim to know me best and therefore had the most cause for anger at me. Just as alarming, I feared the Prince de Conti's hand in this, and to limit the risk of such a shattering potential revelation, I did not mind the Parlement concluding the extended investigation.

I did not hate Damien, nor was I even angry at him. When the Parlement condemned him to the traditional punishment of dismemberment for regicide, I asked for his ordeal to be quickened. But they would not have it. I caught the flash of glazed, enlarged pupils from these unbending, greedy law-keepers in the guise of zeal for the monarchy, repeating no: it would go all the way. I did not insist, lest my care add to their sadistic pleasure.

During his ordeal I knelt in prayer, hoping I looked convincing as I whirled in a storm of sickening stenches and hues—I, a pathetic orphan-king who could not even focus enough to offer a prayerful fight during such a trial! Eventually I ended the day having refused to hear the details of his horrific end.

※

*Guilty, guilty, guilty! How much guiltier is a king! Bring him on the stage!*

I stood on the Place de Grève, somehow able to see far in different directions, all filled with angry crowds turned to me. Feeling naked and exposed, it instantly reminded me of the plays I'd been forced to perform in as a child, and though I tried to run, I was paralyzed.

*No! All the way!*

I saw the disheveled and bloodied Damien confess, and then listen to the mass sung at the Sainte-Chapelle—built by my canonized royal ancestor—and assist in the Benediction of the Blessed Sacrament. Then I was back at the Place de Grève, where the crowds swarmed, clamoring for his release as the guards struggled to hold them back. My throat squeezed as trembling Damien kissed the cross extended to him several times.

That's enough, I said.

*No! All the way!* And I realized it was that voice keeping me in place.

Tied to a low scaffold, they burned his murdering right hand, followed by molten lead, sulfur, molten wax, and boiling oil poured into his tortured seeping wounds. His body sliced like a piece of meat, the first executioner fainted, and I thought it would all end when they could find no one else to replace him. Then a second executioner came, heavily drunk.

That's enough, I repeated, even as I knew I wouldn't move as the four horses were harnessed to his arms and legs. Then the pulling began, but nothing happened, because his limbs wouldn't release. *There, a sign of his goodness; his saintly strength!* I thought I heard someone shout. The whips lashed, the deafening pleading cries competed with his pain, and the more the horses pulled, neighing in defiance, the more I was sure that at last, it would finally end. At last they'd agree with me and see the cruel madness of it, and this terrible tragedy would come to its end right there!

*No! All the way!*

I became aware of at least four hours passing by, and though I tightly shut my eyes, I still saw it—the left thigh that came off first, then the other, and the shoulders. The trunk and the head fell to the floor, and some swore that he was still breathing when they threw all the limbs into the fire to be furthermore transformed to ash.

Enough! I screamed, and to my horror the shrieking grew even louder, all while the magistrates were a mixture of pleased and bored.

*He's like a martyr who bravely sustains pain!*

All the red-black eyes turned on me, and my chest constricted as the crowds pointed at me.

*Nothing! You did nothing!*

I tried! But he knew his fate by attacking me: *lèse majesté!*

*Lèse majesté is for a king who honors his sacred duty! Who are you who sits in his place?*

The orphan-king, to whom they would do the same! It was not my fault, but theirs!

*But it's your Jeanne Antoinette! It's your Unigenitus! It's your weakness!*

Are they? They were imposed on me! *Lèse majesté!*

*But you allow it!*

Who are you to judge me? *Lèse majesté!*

*What would the king have done, if it had been his own daughter!*

I awoke from my nightmare drenched in sweat, then began uncontrollably shaking and sobbing—ashamed that my valet whose cord I had tied to my wrist had to see me in such a sorry state.

Why hadn't I gone, blazed a way through the crowd and demanded them to stop? Even if they wouldn't have listened, it would've been something—a genuine gesture! I wept at the heart-wrenching loss of the opportunity.

Nothing!

So often I'd been glad to avoid bloodshed, but with his death it was as if I'd undone all that. Why hadn't I this once broken my mask of emotional control—merged my forgiveness and pent-up wrath—by *demanding* them to let him go! Why hadn't I believed it before that, despite my fear, they wouldn't have dared to do a thing, let alone to kill me right then? Even with all the defiance, they feared me too much, though they'd never say it!

I should've gone, and been a better father-king they'd expected and needed me to be... But then what? Continue as if none of it had happened? It would never please me to think that perhaps this one instant might temper my kingdom's raging thirst for blood. They might've all wanted me dead, but at least I preferred it coming from Damien, and his harrowing ordeal would maintain its aura of sanctity.

I imagined his family would be more ashamed of me than I of them, with his birthplace razed to the ground, his wife, daughter, and father exiled, and the rest of the family forced to change their name.

Nothing!

Nothing; this storm would pass, as they all had, until the next one God, the Devil, or both wanted me to watch.

But I deserved no rest, for each day added to my unrelenting sorrow with Jeanne Antoinette's mounting suspicion of the Prince de Conti inciting Huguenots in the south to revolt, and I spiraled into such deep uncertainty of my position that I even considered abdicating. But why add to my shame? No matter how much I'd failed my subjects, the least I had to do was go on until the end. I don't know why it took me so long to realize that that's what it means to be a king: everyone wants a piece of you and each time you think you can't take anymore, incredibly you still go on living.

Then, once again, in the heart of my uselessness, appeared a glimmer of hope that I wasn't completely wrong. The intrepid, born-rider Charles-Geneviève returned from Russia, with Empress Elizabeth's agreement to the small business of our secret alliance. Not only was it two days before the arrival of the Empress's other official communication, but my agent had done so despite the long land route, his carriage overturning on the way, and arriving with a broken leg. I rewarded him with a pension, and a gold snuffbox embellished with pearls and my portrait, and after being treated by my surgeon, off he went back.

In the meantime, the Prince de Conti returned to me all documents pertaining to the Secret, and while his role in it was over, I was no less concerned for the independence of Poland. At least, such was my official position, when my new alliance with Russia reminded me all too well of their own interest in Poland, which I wasn't against sacrificing if it benefited us both. Why should I not be ready to take either approach, with so much disloyalty around me! As for the agents, they knew the delicate nature of the work, and while I'd reward their efforts to the best of my ability—as I'd done for years out of my own coffers to avoid detection—I was also ready to disown them at any moment for my security. I liked to think that we were each doing our duty, though I was nearly sure they'd desert me before I did them.

In September my oldest daughter Elisabeth joined us from Parma, and I took solace in her headstrong presence as she attended the negotiations between France and Austria, with her keen eye to any benefit to her husband Philip.

We also shared our discreet amusement at the annual Salon's critics of Boucher for making the Beast look too young and beautiful in her lavish green silk gown and accessories whose details—including her pet spaniel Mimi—were surely more pleasantly truer to life.

The Dauphin had another son, Charles Phillippe, Comte d'Artois, bringing my grandsons through him to four.

It'd been six years since work on the École Militaire had first begun, for which Pâris-Duverney was still in need of funds. With his need, and Jeanne Antoinette's acquaintance, the Venetian Casanova, I was convinced to launch a national lottery to finance it.

As the year came to a close, I tried to take some solace in the English failure to capture our port of Rochefort. Most touching of all was the loyalty displayed to me by my Protestant subjects in La Rochelle. Rather than seeing the approaching English fleet and their impending invasion as liberating—unlike those wanting to leave France—several volunteered to defend our coast. In gratitude, I ordered the removal of the plaques on the gate *des Minimes* commemorating the fall of the city in 1628 as a Huguenot enclave. I wanted, and needed, to remember this mark of friendship, and was a timely reminder that allegiance might not always come from where I'd expect.

This contemplation went right with the anticipated ominous Halley's Comet that many believed had caused the Biblical flood. Though it did not pass by earth as had been predicted, it had certainly been the worst year of my life, though I needed no comet or signs to confirm it.

Our ships faced the English at the indecisive battle of Cap-Français in Saint-Domingue, and a devastating epidemic of typhus broke out among our naval crews in Brest in Brittany, for which I demanded to be kept updated regardless of time, lest the infection spread through the whole region.

Recalling my overdue promise to build a church to house the relics of Saint Geneviève in gratitude for surviving Metz—and now an assassination attempt—I finally ordered the edifice built with designs by architect Soufflot, first sketched a few years before. Located on the hill named after the saint, I took solace in reflecting on our long history, and how Clovis I had constructed a church where he and his wife were later buried, over twelve-hundred years earlier. I was not always pleased with myself, but even I knew there would be some good things I might leave behind for others to remember, too.

If not hunting, wallowing in my private apartments, or keeping my trysts brief for lack of interest, I passed some time perusing Jean Jacques Barthelemy's work. Recommended by Choiseul, the scholar had recently deciphered ancient Phoenician and Palmyrene.

Voltaire published *Candide*, and just from hearing about its rejection of optimism, I surprised myself in not only that I wouldn't read it, but that I disagreed, for even with all my fears and melancholy I knew that had to be wrong. It added to my satisfaction in his short-lasting spell at King Frederick II's court, and for my choice of banning him from Paris years before.

In contrast, his friend Jeanne Antoinette at times still managed to amuse me with her special breed of chickens roaming on the roof, and the eggs she was proud to cook in her jade-colored porcelain vase burner—with a decorative chicken on top—that doubled as a steamer. To continue flaunting her influence, she also sat for another portrait by Boucher in her lavish peach gown in a garden, with even her pet spaniel Inès at her side looking away elsewhere.

They'd already begun, so onwards went Choiseul as he frenetically maneuvered the descent on the English coast, sparing no expense and eager for our French victory without relying on the popular and beloved Bonnie Prince's powers. Bent on speedy action, his vision of a French fleet of 100,000 troops would easily overcome the weak English army and thus kick Britain out of the war. I secretly had little faith in its success, in part due to the incompetence of Berryer—that notoriously hated former chief of police, since turned Secretary of the Navy—with wayward crews lacking sound guidance and discipline that fueled high rates of desertion.

The storm raged, but for the first time in my life I watched it with painless, even amused detachment. The delayed—or timely!—worrisome passing of Halley's Comet; our maritime defeats at Lagos and Quiberon Bay that marred our plans to invade; the battle of Quebec; rising challenges to our colonies in India; even the capture of our Guadeloupe sugar island...

They were all mine, no matter what happened or whose hands they ended up in! I had been certain of little in life, but that year, as the misery unfurled and came for us, I knew I was stronger than all those who'd tried and would continue to attack me. For I'd come upon the greatest man-made power I'd ever encountered, and though every part of me screamed to resort to it, I did not.

A chemist from Dauphiné named André Dupré informed me of his chance discovery of how to make a new Greek fire. As much as I doubted its truth, I had him secretly reveal his experiment at Versailles and Belleville, and on the coasts at Le Havre and Dunkirk.

As the unrelenting flames roared, I knew then that what we imagine could never compare to its reality. It was greater and more terrifying than I could've thought, but in that moment I wallowed in the golden storm, merging with Saturn and Vesuvius in wanting it all to explode, to blast all these greedy nobles, clerics, financiers, magistrates, and all other ungrateful subjects to hell—or anywhere else, so long as it was far away from me! And perhaps I'd finally have my private, quiet kingdom with endless time to spend alone as I so needed and sought!

But the rotting stench filled my chest and I thought of all the victims of the wars, the plague of Marseille, and the Lisbon earthquake whose circumstances still left us speechless, and I was consumed with shame to be so selfish and childish in my self-righteousness. As vicious as our enemies could be, I did not want them to use such an inhumane weapon on us, so how could I use it on them? I knew part of it was once more my paralyzing fear of hell, and even if I was still destined for it, at least it wouldn't be for using that vile trick. There was another vanity, as surely I had several forms, but I wanted us to succeed the right way from our civilized talents, not from resorting to a cheating tool. Just as well, I fantasized that my ring of secret spies might bring us success that would better prove my perceptive abilities and diplomatic skills.

Strangely, as I ruminated I had a sense of euphoria. A weight lifted off me as if my time of obsessing over every little detail and scenario had passed, and might not even be necessary, or even possible...! It felt as if it'd been a long test, and though I hadn't done as well as I'd wanted, I hadn't totally failed it either. Because despite it all, there I remained—suggesting God hadn't completely deserted me, and I was still worthy of living another day in this kingdom envied and lauded by the world...

Swallowing my emotion, I decided to forbid the use of this terrible weapon and paid off Dupré for his silence with money and a noble title. Thus few knew I'd exchanged wrath for a harrowing piece of knowledge that I still wish none of us had known. And as I saw once more the greed of always wanting more—a desperate feeling I knew too well—it soothed me to know that even mine had limits.

The Dauphin welcomed a daughter, Marie Clotilde, as sister to his four sons, and Elisabeth planned the marriage of her oldest daughter Isabelle to Archduke Joseph of Austria. Caron, now titled de Beaumarchais, also became harp instructor to Mesdames, and had become close friends with Pâris-Duverney, with the welcomed development that the École Militaire was near completion.

I hunted, and tried to pass some time with my new mistresses Marguerite-Catherine, who soon fell pregnant, and Lucie Madeleine. It was only natural for me to rotate my interests as any pregnant mistress required distance.

Then my heart was stabbed into once more, when Elisabeth fell ill and died of smallpox in winter, seven years after her twin. I shed bitter tears, envious of my twins who were now reunited, as I recalled first holding this precious pair who'd made me a father at seventeen. Before

I could stop myself, my tears redoubled at the thought of Nattier's paintings of them as half of the four elements. I didn't care what it looked like in hindsight! I refused to think of them as ominous signs of the fire that had first been snuffed out with Henriette, and now the earth symbolized by Elisabeth to cruelly suggest I was about to lose that, too... Of my ten children with the Queen, there now remained five.

I surely didn't need Halley's Comet to fuel my neverending fears, but as I reflected on all the year's devastating events, I couldn't decide if it was better or worse than my assassination attempt just two years earlier. A gaping, angry black hole stretched in me as I reluctantly sensed an irreparable global shift in favor of the English, and one that we may not overcome, or at least not without great strain.

I thought of Louis XIV and all the heirs he lost, reminding me that I might suffer a similar fate. Mostly, I feared the Bull *Unigenitus* causing more division, and wondered if he'd truly still stand by it if he were in my place. The question seemed to possess me as I paced back and forth, with whispers competing with each other for my attention, and the one direct tone that stood out amongst them all—and before I knew it it'd been at least two hours that I'd reflected on it. I hoped it wasn't just my wishful thinking, but a guiding sign from Louis XIV as I surprisingly, even hesitatingly, concluded that he'd also changed his mind, filling me with ease to release my own wavering grip on it.

Soon after I met an Amazonian brunette beauty—relayed to me through Casanova and my trusted Lebel—who, much to my humbled shock, showed me that I could still fall deeply in love. Anne de Roman was the daughter of a lawyer from Grenoble whose colossal perfection had me awestruck. She had such a natural ease about her that I needed to merge with it and create a new romance that would finally differ from the repetitive, temporary others.

It delighted me all the more that she had demands that separated her from the rest. For one, she refused to join the others at the Parc-aux-Cerfs, so I gave her her own house in Passy, playfully called l'Hôtel de la Folie, with a carriage drawn by six horses to bring her to Versailles. Eventually came the title Baronesse de Meilly-Coulonge. I was so in love that I was emboldened and unworried about showing my love that might frustrate the Beast, who I increasingly hoped would be whisked away by her frail health.

In partial hopes of expediting that outcome, I bought the precious Sèvres factory, thus rendering it "royal," for as much as she might've become its major patron, it'd only been possible because of me.

I breathed a bit easier, too, when Charles-Geneviève returned once more from Russia after four years away, for which I rewarded him with another pension. Wanting to prove himself further, I granted his wish to elevate from the honorific Lieutenant General title to Captain of Dragoons, and he joined the ongoing war effort on the Prussian front with Maréchal de Broglie. With some kingly-fatherly pride, it pleased me to see such brave dedication from a subject willing to serve me with deep secrets that stretched across such long distances.

In the guise of politeness, I said I trusted he'd received memorable trinkets from his stay in Russia as well. I had to suppress a satisfied chuckle when he revealed that Empress Elizabeth also gave him a gold snuffbox encrusted with diamonds and her image—amusing me that he'd acquired this royal pair in our secret service. If nothing else, some-day he'd have some stories to tell on how he'd come about such prized treasures.

We once again rallied around the Dauphin when his oldest son, Louis, the Duc de Bourgogne, began to limp and, upon examination, was revealed to have a tumor on his thigh. I shared the Dauphin's frustration as the doctors argued over how to proceed, reminding me yet again that their advanced knowledge didn't necessarily ease decision-making in worrisome situations.

They decided on a surgery to remove the tumor, and the Duc pleasantly surprised me with his resolve in first reviewing the operating tools, as if wisely soothing his fears before getting on the procedure. Why do we think that strength comes with age? For I was the one most horrified as I watched the favorite of his parents being cut into like a willing prey while he was fully awake, and bravely endured the pain with barely a few cries.

The operation didn't seem to help when he became paler and soon had to use a wheelchair and became increasingly bedridden. He was diagnosed with bone consumption and, showing little sign of recovery, the Dauphin decided to baptize him, with myself and the Queen as his godparents. He died soon after, and I shed more shattering tears for this fifth lost grandson, as I recalled all the long-awaited celebrations I'd ordered for Paris less than a decade before. I prayed and begged God with all my heart that his three brothers would be spared the same fate.

Our affairs remained just as unstable, when Empress Elizabeth suggested a bold treaty alliance between our two kingdoms without informing Austria. Though I wasn't against the possibility of reconciling with Britain in exchange for harsher fighting against Prussia, I worried about offending the Ottoman Porte. Most difficult to admit was my jealousy at Russia's mounting power in Eastern Europe, and as tempting as it sounded, I couldn't help but wonder what else she might be planning with Austria without informing me.

In search of support, rather than suing Britain and its allies for peace, Choiseul advised reversing Spain's previous policy and convincing them to join us as an ally in the war. Ever hopeful for new discoveries beneficial to us, I also supported the explorer Marion Du Fresne in his voyage to the Indian Ocean, with astronomer Alexandre Gui Pingré as companion to observe the transit of Venus.

After the mourning time had passed, Adélaïde and Victoire visited the waters in Lorraine for their health, and Sophie and Louise visited Paris for the first time. Like Marguerite-Catherine, my mistress Lucie Madeleine also gave birth to a girl, but more importantly, in my love for Anne de Roman, I agreed to legitimize her son, Louis Aimé. However, it was on the conditions that his birth remain a secret unless confessed to a priest, and that his godparents be either poor or servants.

I did not mind—and in a way even wanted!—that it would cause a stir since it was not only the first time I'd ever agreed to do this, but also with a non-noble born woman. Best of all, it would worry the Beast, whose time I wished would end sooner rather than later. In my genuine love for Anne, and the kingdom, I considered my own lingering fear that my heir could meet his end at any moment—as we all could. I prayed my new undertaking was an extreme, even unnecessary precaution, and as I thought of Charles, whose mother Pauline Félicité never truly left my thoughts, at least we were both of noble blood no matter my official stance.

On days when my mind was a drained blur, I thanked God that He knew the truth and would account for all my wayward doings, should I unconsciously—or conveniently—forget my long and expanding list of women and illegitimate children.

At the news of Empress Elizabeth's death, I shed some secret tears too, as much for our tentative, though limited interactions as for what might've been. After all these years of establishing an alliance, I fretted about maintaining our Franco-Russian relations, as her heir and nephew Peter III's admiration for Frederick II did not look promising for us. As such I called back Charles-Geneviève—who'd since earned a brave reputation—from the front, to be ready should he be needed to intervene in the *Secret*.

Eager for more promising embellishment, I ordered architect Gabriel to begin work on the Petit Trianon for Jeanne Antoinette, hoping that it would go to Anne de Roman instead.

The Dauphin had another stillborn son—his fourth—and Marguerite-Catherine birthed another girl. Given my infatuation with Anne, I saw fit to end this relation and award Marguerite-Catherine with a pension for herself and the two daughters she'd birthed in two years.

Charles-Geneviève was on the verge of returning to Saint Petersburg with an impressive crew when we heard of Catherine overthrowing her husband Peter III. It was yet another reminder of how quickly things could change. As such, I had to renege on my previous agreement to him becoming French ambassador in Stockholm, when this post he'd anticipated proved no longer vacant. He was not the only one disappointed when, despite our efforts, I concluded that the war had to end once and for all, forcing me to sue the English for peace. Instead I consoled him with another pension and order to accompany the Duc de Nivernais in order to draft the peace treaty for this Seven Years' War.

We signed the Treaty of Paris soon after, in what was a crushing blow for us to the great delight of our English enemy. In the course of the war, they'd ruined our navy and taken the bulk of our colonial possessions in Canada, the West Indies, the shores of Senegal, and our factories in India. We were returned Guadeloupe, Martinique, Saint Lucia, the coasts of Senegal, and Pondicherry in exchange for ceding Canada and the other West Indies islands. They also received Spanish Florida, while we'd already secretly previously agreed to give Louisiana to Spain, to whom we were at least related to by Bourbon blood.

While I saw the prized sugar island of Guadeloupe as more valuable than Canada, I fumed at the loss of our New France territories. The area east of the Mississippi went to the English, and the western part to Spain to compensate for its loss of Florida. What nightmarish shame! What would Louis XIV say! To have come so far, only to become just another weak kingdom in the eyes of our Indian allies! I tried to console myself with what we were able to keep, convincing myself that doing otherwise would've been even worse.

But my anger would not relent this time.

*Will you finally use it now, or let it slip away again!*

It taunted me, and in the putrid black pit I was trapped in danced the new Greek fire once more, its flames writhing like enticing exotic women donned in golden ermine... Would I—recall that chemist and undo what I did, to do what I should've done in the first place? All the good and self-sacrifice I'd done would surely excuse—if not demand!—this course of action.

Then there was a flash of light, sparking the simple truth: that I'd rather have little than nothing at all.

As I pondered this devastating outcome, I came back to the same thing: the harmful decisions the Beast, Choiseul, and the rest of her entourage had made. So was it really my fault, when I handed over the reins, if partly in hopes to show that birth didn't always have to mean everything! Even if I was the only one to know the extent of it, she'd repeatedly proven that her kind's place was not in politics, and that no amount of ambition and even greed equaled success. I tried to decipher what she'd truly wanted out of this, and a part of me was left stunned that if it'd been her goal to ruin us, she'd played her part exceedingly well.

My desire for revenge lingered, and in gratitude to Charles-Geneviève for his work, he received another pension, the Order of Saint Louis, and the title of Chevalier d'Éon. Back in London, he eventually became plenipotentiary minister in the Duc de Nivernais' absence. His task was to keep spying and gather information for our overdue descent on the English coast.

Meanwhile, the statue of myself by Bouchardon as a Roman general on horseback as victor of the Battle of Fontenoy was inaugurated on Place Louis XV. A part of me wanted to be angry at the mockery that followed, while another couldn't fully disagree in light of my own disappointments.

Our ongoing desperate need for money had me trust in the advice of Quesnay—my trusted doctor and also celebrated economic theorist—to allow the free circulation of grains. Traditionally under strict control by the Jesuits, they believed it would increase production, competition, and lower prices.

De Gournay, who was the Minister of the Commerce of the King, and Quesnay's disciple, echoed his support in saying *laissez faire*; let it pass, suggesting it would not only resolve the crisis, but enrich the peasants in the process. I hesitated with this new liberal idea, when the traditionally fixed price of bread was linked to its sacred nature and the king's fatherly role of providing. Though I disagreed with their dismissal of these religious views, deemed superstitions and expired in our times of expanding knowledge and new ideas, our dire situation made me conclude that it had to be worth trying.

That year, Charles-Amédée Van Loo displayed his allegorical portrait of myself at the Salon to great success. At first glance, the image reveals six figures: Justice, surrounded by Magnanimity, Military Valor, Heroic Courage, Minerva, and Generosity. But it was only by looking at it with the required faceted lens, that my face would appear on the crest at center, made of pieces from the surrounding elements. Though I liked to think that all of these said virtues made up a part of me, it pained me that the faces of Medusa and the Mask were most familiar.

I mourned the loss of my oldest grandchild Isabelle, who passed away in Vienna of smallpox four years after her mother Elisabeth. My heart broke for this sweet twenty-two-year-old who'd grieved her mother's passing, an unhappy marriage, and several miscarriages. Despite their personal troubles, she was loved by her husband Joseph of Austria, to whom she left a one-year-old daughter Maria Theresa, and several intelligent writings.

I distracted myself by wishfully thinking of Bougainville's ongoing journey to find and conquer the Falkland Islands in the South Atlantic, and all the discoveries he'd bring us back.

Soon after I also had occasion to be impressed by a young Austrian composer invited by the Queen, aged only seven or eight. I would've liked to tell this Mozart not to be vexed when the Beast vainly snubbed his wish for an embrace—as if she hadn't once been a non-noble herself! It was but one reminder of the way these lowest kinds can exceed the haughtiness of any noble-born. But the prodigy instantly had reason to set it aside when Victoire, the Queen, and everyone else showered him with due love. He dazzled them all in Victoire's room, playing the harpsichord as if he'd done so since he was born. Mozart also found his lack of French remedied in the Queen who easily spoke

German with him and his family. He composed and dedicated his first sonata to Victoire, and his second to the Comtesse de Tessé, and earned a small pension for it.

Was there something about me that made others want to turn on me, or was it an uncomfortable truth that humans would just inevitably betray each other? Still in London, Charles-Geneviève had taken to spending wild sums of money that wasn't his; namely by hosting luxurious dinners—complete with his wine imported from Tonnerre—to which all the highest of London society came, including King George III. If nothing else, I envied him that, when it was that very endearing ability of his to see—and be seen by—others as an equal that had first made me think I could trust him. As grateful as I was for his service, I could not let him drain the already strained coffers.

As a humbling lesson to him, I sent the Comte de Guerchy, supported by Choiseul and the Beast, to demote him to secretary. Almost instantly, my secret agent made it clear that he wasn't getting on with his superior de Guerchy, even if I knew it was partially because of his hurt pride at the self-induced demotion. Why couldn't he be grateful to still be in my service, no matter what that looked like? For the first time, he'd disobeyed my orders of returning to France and, as a perpetual reminder that the English would always be ready to side against me, their government refused my request to extradite him. Could I still trust him when he claimed that de Guerchy had tried to poison him, or was it part of his antics to get more out of me? I had little choice but to stop his pension.

And there, I had the scandalous surprise of my life, when he did what no one else dared to do before: he published our secret correspondence about his recall to France that lampooned de Guerchy's incompetence. I panicked, repelled by his audacity even as I envied it, and hated that he held me in the palm of his hand by holding back our crucial invasion documents. How many reminders would I get in this unrelenting, tormenting life of mine?! Each time that I thought things couldn't get worse, I was shown otherwise.

De Guerchy sued for libel, and though Charles-Geneviève was declared an outlaw and went into hiding, it only served to make him more popular and beloved by the public. Perhaps it'd been my fault for thinking that secret affairs might be more reliable than official ones, though I'd never faced such a bold situation before. I considered having him kidnapped before he could betray me worse than he already had, but that seemed impossible, especially since he was likely to be more closely watched. In the meantime, the best course of action seemed to leave him to his fate and keep my distance, and see what time might reveal.

As if an undeserved attempt to cheer me up, at last, the moment I'd awaited for so long… The Beast breathed her last and finally left! The first movement of Vivaldi's "Spring" symphony echoed in my elated soul, promising this most flourishing season without her! Indeed, God is the master and we must all surrender to his wishes—I'd never felt this more strongly than I did then!

Oh, how I easily feigned my sadness as I looked out the balcony into the cold and rainy Marble Courtyard. I found it perfectly representative of the nearly twenty years of anguish she gave me, countered by what I hoped was the glorious renewal this baptismal storm would bring. Surely even our chickens were celebrating by laying extra eggs! Finished—No more of her spying on Anne de Roman as she showed off Louis at the Bois de Boulogne; no more of her fretting, claiming to remain at court only for my well-being! She was buried with her daughter Alexandrine, who'd died nearly a decade before, and I wasn't sure if it was too cruel or right to think that they might not be reunited in the beyond.

To add to my relief, the Dauphin had another daughter, Elisabeth, bringing his flock to three sons and two daughters. For the first time in twelve years, I had the urge to commission Bachelier for three bizarre deer antler pieces, reminiscent of and yet distinct from my beloved ones by Oudry. The first features a shorter set of antlers at the edge of a shelf against a blue-grey background. It makes for a tense effect as the weight of the full, hand-like antlers at left hold it in place, while the other misshapen side contorts and hangs off the ledge. The second painting has an uneven set of antlers nailed against a wall, and the third a full yet deformed set hung up by rope. If I was bold enough I would've mounted it and turned it into a crown... Who would see it? But oh, who wouldn't! But I already knew that I shouldn't give every tormented thought yet another material body.

In the fall, the admiral and explorer Bougainville, whose crew included Dom Pernety, returned from their expedition to the Falkland Islands in the South Atlantic. Having held a formal ceremony of possession on the island and named Port Louis after myself, I was pleased to formally ratify its possession.

I let myself get lost in Messier's trajectory charts and maps of comets, feeling almost like a spy who wasn't supposed to know where they were heading. Surely they had their own unpredictable natures, too, and these were educated guesses. But there was something about looking at his drawings of astronomical animals that made me happy and full of child-like wonder. But then, at times I saddened that if anything else was looking down on us, their curiosity might soon be replaced by aversion at what they saw.

The mathematician Montucla returned from an expedition to Cayenne with the Chevalier Turgot, and offered us several plants from his travels to cultivate in our vegetable gardens of Versailles and Trianon. They included cacao, vanilla, a sweet bean, and a red lentil that the Queen so enjoyed that it was instantly named *lentille à la reine*.

With the Beast gone, I did for a while enjoy spending more time with the Queen, though I did not abandon Anne de Roman—as haughty as she was becoming—or the other less meaningful dalliances that pleased me. Though the court often wondered if Anne would replace the Beast, she was by no means the only one vying for the position, nor was I in a hurry to fill it. Among them was none other than Choiseul's own unattractive sister, Béatrix, and the childish eighteen-year-old Louise-Jeanne, who'd just birthed me a son,

Benoît-Louis. A month after, Lucie Madeleine birthed me another daughter, reminding me that girls were prominent even among my non-official mistresses.

Would I ever be truly master of any decision as king? For I was not fully myself when I let Choiseul—supported for years by the Beast and the Parlement—force me to decree that the Jesuits were banished from France for being dangerous to the state. How quickly things had changed, when some of its most ardent critics like Voltaire and Diderot among them, had benefited from their superior colleges! They were the whining children who constantly demanded their way, yet dared to call me the despot! Though I agreed with the pro-Jesuit Queen and my children on this unfortunate issue, I saw no other option than to go against my wish in hopes of placating the Parlement, and watch them go with heavy a heart to welcoming Prussia and Russia.

My concern deepened when in the fall news spread of horrifying attacks happening to peasants in the remote southern region of Gévaudan. Terror took hold as they seemed to happen mostly to lone women and children while they tended flocks in the fields and forests, leaving bodies torn apart and sometimes even heads ripped off. With the high number of attacks, there were even suspicions that it was several wreaking carnage nearly at once.

I instantly thought of famished wolves, and yet they'd repeatedly said it was no such creature, and even seemed to have supernatural strength. A knot formed in my stomach as some even spoke of hellish werewolf. But learned men easily mocked it, reasoning that in their fear and superstitious beliefs, they surely exaggerated what they saw, and perhaps even for personal gain.

Wolves were bad enough of a threat, and for a moment I wondered if the English had been right in their recent extermination of them all from their land. I shuddered at the thought of Courtaud, that monstrous man-eating wolf who'd left the peak of the Roman Mount of Mars, to roam outside the Paris walls in insatiable search of prey in the 15th century. Or Bisclavret from Brittany, who'd vanish for three days due to his werewolf condition, only to end up trapped in that form due to his wife's uncomfortably familiar treachery... I dreaded that increased deaths from seasonal shortages, war, and disease might've turned some of our wolves towards unnatural taste for human flesh.

With the *Courrier d'Avignon*'s harrowing reports that fueled others, the case was soon talked about everywhere, including London and even Boston and Quebec. As the gruesome attacks continued, it was the twelve-year-old Jacques Portefaix's bravery that finally convinced me to send help to wipe out this monster. Together with his six friends, they fended off the menacing creature, and I was moved to offer him a pension and education at our expense, as well as a pension to be shared among his companions. I resolved to send Captain Duhamel of the Clermont Prince Dragoons and his troops to settle the matter.

Meanwhile, Adélaïde informed me of Venetian playwright Carlo Goldoni's plight with the deteriorating *Comédie-Italienne*, so he was made Italian tutor to Mesdames, whom the Dauphin also appreciated.

If the Gévaudan situation wasn't enough, my blood nearly froze when I heard of such a threat nearly at my doorstep: a man-eating wolf roaming Soissons, close to my beloved Compiègne. After two days of attacking eighteen people, Antoine Saverelle, a former local militiaman, tracked and killed the monster, for which I rewarded him with a pension.

As time passed I was speechlessly annoyed at the fruitless efforts of Duhamel. How could the creature evade what had to be the historically—and embarrassingly—largest hunting party of at least twenty thousand men! Ironically, the increasing stories, and even hand-colored gruesome drawings published by the *Gazette de France* in Paris so fueled the frenzy and obsession that we might've as well been in Gévaudan. Once more, the English lost no time in using that as fodder for more mockery against me.

A spectacular reward was set up for anyone able to catch the monster, which drew a range of eager hunters from different regions. But even the professional wolf hunting father-son duo named d'Enneval from Normandy failed at the promising endeavor.

Frustrated, I sent in my own trusted gunbearer, François Antoine, requesting nothing less than positive results. I half considered going there myself, amused at the idea of leading this hunt that I'd surely triumph at—when I so often felt I succeeded at little else. But I had to show that my entourage was skilled and able to handle this affair.

I even contemplated finally visiting Marie-Angélique, the now middle-aged wild woman who might know what to do about this elusive creature. Suddenly, the strange book by the Lorraine-native monk Dom Calmet, about spirits, vampires, and other strange mysteries sounded less far-fetched. With all the cruelty and indifference in the world, the more amazed I was to think about her having survived alone. Perhaps being alone was a shield of its own... Or what if, in compensation for her lone Eve state, God had gifted her with the magic ability of taming any ferocity?

I imagined going to her apartment on Rue St. Antoine, across the old Rue du Temple, hoping she preferred this new meagre arrangement, even if smaller, than missing the convent. I'd say I trusted that the story written by Mme Hecquet about her life had helped inform and generate sympathy—and maybe even a humble income—for her situation in the ten years since its publication. I wouldn't say that I thought it wrong for the book to advertise her as some exotic animal to be visited and peered at, when surely she knew it even if she didn't protest.

I was certain that she wouldn't agree with Gabriel-Florent, the Bishop of Mende in Gévaudan—and cousin to my prime minister the Duc the Choiseul—saying that it was sent as a scourge of God. As if we weren't suffering enough from the disastrous outcome of the Seven Years' War! What about liberalizing the circulation of grain that was driving up the cost of bread? But I was told it would get better; we only had to wait and see that more "freeing of the market" would prove fruitful! In the pit of my soul I felt like Marie-Angélique would laugh at us, and I would join her in that, too, in our attempts to control everything, only to end up short-handed.

*You don't need as much as you think; when His eternal spark outlasts it all…*

Had she said this? Oh—how I wished she did, and was secretly communicating it to me now, when I most needed it! Before I could drop like a weeping old man, I sniffed away my tears, grateful once more to know that she was near as we both aged and longed for uninterrupted solitude.

My son-in-law Philip, Duc de Parma, died unexpectedly, and thus rejoined his wife who was my oldest child, Elisabeth, and their daughter Isabelle. At least one of his last gestures had been to accompany his daughter Maria Luisa on her way to Genoa, where she sailed for Spain to marry Infante Charles.

It was easy to think that being surrounded by youthful childishness might fend off some of the effects of time. Though it had initially amused me in Louise-Jeanne, she grew haughty, going so far as to toss diamonds I'd gifted her out the window—which I'd consider doing with her as well. Worst of all, she took to pressuring me to recognize our son Benoît-Louis, surely with some inspiration from friends. As if I would easily repeat what I'd done with Anne de Roman! Unrelenting as she was, I had her confined to the Bastille to teach her a lesson, and released less than a month later with a higher pension than she probably deserved.

Would I never learn? But how could I stop myself from falling in love, when contrary to what some might think, I rarely experienced it. I could bear with Anne de Roman in her pride for our son whom she loved to parade around. As ill-mannered as that was, her offensive defiance to the fussy court amused me. But her own deepening arrogance, already trying, turned into yet another blade in my heart when she became implicated in the affair of La Chalotais. Like so many others, this unpleasant jurist from the Parlement of Brittany, with writings predictably fawned over by Voltaire, saw fit to challenge my authority over a taxation issue. This betrayal from Anne was more than I could bear. I ordered Louis Aimé taken away from her, and ended my relation with her, though not without leaving her with the largest pension I'd ever given any mistress from the Parc-aux-Cerfs. I shunned love and, wishing to be alone, would keep as basic account of her wedding and whereabouts as possible.

I welcomed better news when on the first day of October, François Antoine's slain, dissected, and mounted wolf of Chazes was presented at court. For a small fee, visitors thronged in and out of the Queen's antechambers to behold the large wolf… but a simple wolf nonetheless. As François Antoine collected my monetary gratitude and the public's accolades, I wavered between satisfaction and disappointment at this creature that had also contributed to tarnishing my image.

*No! All the way!*

I shook off the disgusting sneer that rattled down my spine, and consoled myself with the proof that it hadn't been anything extraordinary or paranormal after all. Then, for a moment, I wondered why we'd even allowed this hellish creature into the palace—and in the superstitious Queen's quarters, lest its vile essence make its home among us… but then realized it was just the usual stress and tension preying upon me.

So many children gone… and yet at least I prayed that none of mine would ever succumb by being ripped apart by a raged animal. But I'd seen it nonetheless; the way my corpulent son the Dauphin had gradually lost weight and turned pale. Was that not a monster too, miniscule and lurking somewhere inside of him, that none of us could track and stop? The physicians whose remedies didn't work… In my helplessness I thought that passing time with Cassini de Thury in astronomical calculations, we might come upon some unexpected solution.

For a month, I watched him slip away, even as I hoped something would change at the last moment. Nothing ever certain, not even that stuffed and mounted wolf of Chazes, when after only a brief respite, the attacks resumed. Was the Dauphin thinking it too, or did it all look absurd in light of his next eternal mission? Was the wrong creature killed—the right target so often missed?

Of all the reminders of my helplessness, that of his peaceful resolve was most humbling. He was going ahead of me, to a better place! My good, strict son: he could have that consolation, unlike me. How I envied his faith, he who'd lost his beloved first wife, had five stillborn children, and four who'd died in childhood! Could he forgive me, he who didn't seem afraid of anything? So much, so much I'd wanted to say over the years—but it was not meant to be... Or, I preferred to think, perhaps not yet.

After a month of agonizing, he went early in the morning, ceding his thirty-six-year role of Dauphin to his eleven-year-old, Louis Auguste. And I fled to Choisy to drown in my tears.

My vision blurred anew as I lingered on the portraits Alexandre Roslin had just made of my Dauphin as an equestrian, and his half-length pastel portrait with his blue sash of the Order of the Holy Spirit. But the hardest to look at was his half-portrait of him as a colonel of his own regiment of dragoons, standing in the camp near the Compiègne residence. While Roslin succeeded in making him look as appealing as possible despite his weight loss, in my warring sad-angry-resolved emotions, I could easily add some weight to his frame in our mutual appreciation for quality fare.

Adélaïde and Victoire also had their Roslin portraits anonymously displayed at the Salon, and while Diderot had plenty of rude comments to say about both the subjects and the rendition—as if he were an undisputed authority on art and good taste—all that mattered was that my daughters were entirely satisfied.

I also thought of my twenty-four-year-old son Charles with Pauline Félicité, and how ashamed I felt. By turns I wallowed in regret for not recognizing him, while no one knew better than his mother and I that we both have noble blood. Perhaps if I'd reached out to him while I was still beloved by my subjects, he would've been proud and desirous enough to openly want me as his father. What was I now, but a philandering king who kept losing—his children, his territories, his subjects' love and loyalty. I clung to what I could, and forced myself to think it was enough for me to know that he had a promising military career in Corsica, and had recently married.

Back at Versailles after the new year, I shared my will, pleading to God and all I'd offended for forgiveness and expressing my Catholic faith. If nothing else could be granted, I prayed that my plea might be heard for my grandchildren to be guided and reign better than I had. I also took note of the limited mourning for my son, and if I'd been in a different mood, I might've reacted violently to Choiseul's barely suppressed rejoicing at my departed Jesuit-admiring Dauphin. I was well aware that it might be a glimpse into my own fate, but I derived satisfaction from trusting the fact that, no matter my wrongs, they were not my divine judge.

Our mourning was added to with the passing of the Queen's father Stanislas, who succumbed to his wounds after his nightgown caught fire. The eighty-four-year-old was mourned by the whole of Lorraine, which, along with the duchy of Bar, passed to France as previously stipulated.

I paced in my private apartments, taking side-glances at my hunting scenes. The shadow of death hung over me, and I wondered why I hadn't thought of it sooner.

*Gévaudan! J'ai vos dents! I have your teeth!*

How it'd begun so soon after the Beast's passing—and the first victim was a fourteen-year-old girl named Jeanne... Was that her twisted revenge, another attempt at control from the beyond? She who'd had my teeth, my speech, but not my mind! No, not that, and why hide when she'd been the accomplished peacock? Or—was this retribution for what had happened to Pauline Félicité's body; the way bodies were savagely mutilated, sometimes with limbs and even heads never recovered... How long, before the Deceiver would come out into the light? My thoughts raced, as I recalled something Captain Duhamel had said about its father being a lion... and I regretted that some things may have been lost between the sights, descriptions, drawings, and sensationalist publications.

I gave Bougainville permission to circumnavigate the globe, and granted Charles-Geneviève a pension to keep him quiet in London, but refused to clear his substantial debts. Perhaps we had a truce of sorts, for if I could not have our compromising letters, neither could he return to his beloved France.

I commissioned two more bizarre deer antler paintings from Bachelier; one with its antlers facing in different directions, and the other with balanced antlers hanging against a wall.

Three summers after the *Gévaudan* creature was first reported, one of their local hunters named Jean Chastel killed a creature from Ténazeyre during a hunt with the local nobleman, Marquis d'Apcher. I was informed that he came to Versailles to present it, but was dismissed for its deplorable condition exasperated by the summer heat. Despite my lingering ambivalence, I'd like to think it was the creature in question, when the attacks stopped thereafter. I prayed for his forgiveness in not acknowledging his achievement, and for the hundreds who'd died or been harmed. Though a mostly Catholic region, I also prayed for any Protestants or others who may have perished and not been recorded, as per Catholic protocol.

The Dauphin's wife, Maria Josepha, who'd never recovered from my son's passing, followed him a little over a year later, dying of the same disease of consumption. My heart tore for my five grandchildren who were now without both parents, as were my other two grandchildren from my oldest daughter Elisabeth. I prayed for the mourning Queen to have some consolation as work finally began on the Queen's Convent of the Augustines, to serve as a boarding school for young girls. First envisioned after the death of her father, it was entrusted to Richard Mique, an architect from Lorraine.

For a while I had had some consolation in Adélaïde de Bullioud, Comtesse de Séran, with whom I had a close, yet chaste idyll. Her beauty and modesty by turns appeased me and reminded me of my own sinful shortcomings. Then, for once, the past pleasantly resurged with la Belle Morphise, who had been forced to leave twelve years before. Since then, her first husband had died, and with her second husband being a distant cousin to the Beast's husband, I found it amusing that Morphise ironically became related to the one who'd most wanted her gone. Our first daughter, Agathe Louise, was nearing thirteen, and I relished discreetly resuming my flame for my thirty-year-old Irish beauty.

In London, Charles-Geneviève continued to steer attention to himself, and as yet another mark that others often seemed to have better luck on their side than I, the trial for libel came to an end with de Guerchy's death. I thought this would placate him, as it somewhat did myself, for I was never certain that I could trust de Guerchy—so aligned with Choiseul—with my secret personal politics. But once again, the Chevalier could not restrain himself, when he had to publish a fiery pamphlet aptly titled, *Last Letter to M. Guerchy*, as if sure to exonerate himself of all guilt with the last word. Wasn't it enough that de Guerchy had perished under a horse's hooves, as symbolic—and perhaps even fitting—as we both might've considered it? Even in this case, I had to admire his unbending defiance, when he knew as well as I that Versailles would be scandalized by an impoverished noble breaching protocol by insulting a higher-ranking nobleman.

There was little else I wanted done—or could hope for—than for him to stay put in London, and report on some potentially useful secret information. Though it was not the egregious sum he wanted, at least he was assisted by the money I'd recently reluctantly agreed to provide him. While I was grateful for the work he'd done, he could still cause damage, and worse, bring us into another war with Britain. Despite his audacity, I could not bring myself to think that he would go so far as treason. He could keep teasing with his charades and self-satisfaction that fueled his popularity and the English pamphlets published out of Grub Street against me, but we both knew that none of these things could grant him safe passage home.

Mesdames were assigned a new reader, Madame Campan, and I dallied with some interests as I awaited la Belle Morphise to conclude her pregnancy. Early in the year, she birthed me a second daughter, Marguerite Victoire, but my flame was soon turned elsewhere when I met another beauty named Jeanne Bécu. The twenty-five-year-old married and titled Venus had me under her spell... all thanks to her unsurpassed intimate talents that made me feel once more like a young man! I liked to think it was meant as a balm for my old sixty years and all the loneliness and romantic failures. Her presence soothed and flattered me, even if I was still a handsome king who'd always be sought after by endless insatiable subjects.

The truth remained that gradually, half of me was slipping away, too, as the Queen's dejection deepened after the loss of her father, her son, and daughter-in-law. Ever the pious and charitable Queen, she withdrew from court and visited churches, while our thirty-five-year-old Adélaïde increasingly appeared in her place. When the Queen was diagnosed with a tumor in the chest, for months I hardly left her side, listened to the doctors and any information I could, as I watched each day slip away the last ties of our married life.

Her passing was a perfect reflection of her life: quiet and restrained, with her rosary in her hand, the day after her sixty-fifth birthday. Forty-three years of marriage, and six children of ten—gone. The irreparable loss and remorse filled me, a familiar shattering sense that I could never elevate while others progressed. And at last she wouldn't have to worry about me anymore; her baby-husband requiring pathetic, lustful satisfaction! The king who, the more he tried to find other ways to make things right, only seemed to make them worse. As she deserved, she'd be instantly greeted in heaven, with a procession even more impressive than that of her burial—and without all the black and somber draperies. She was buried at Saint-Denis, and as per her wish, her heart went to the crypt of Notre-Dame-de-Bonsecours in Nancy, next to her parents Catherine and Stanislas.

In contrast to all my failings, the Queen had been beloved for her genuine faith and charity, and I quivered at the worrying rising price of grain that too many couldn't afford. It even fueled some rumors that there was a deliberate plot to starve the poor, and I prayed to them all—my wife, my son, *maman* Ventadour, Pauline Félicité, Cardinal Fleury, surgeon Mareschal, and all the saints to intercede for me to Jesus for it to promptly pass.

Aside from her talents for rejuvenating me, Jeanne Bécu also had a natural charm coupled with high spirits and good humor that delightfully made her stand out from court. Though pleasure was a significant factor, it was mostly her unpretentious personality and my loneliness that drove my decision to make her an official mistress.

My unexpected commitment alarmed Lebel, who then informed me of her true past as a commoner and prostitute. I raged at this vile lie that suggested I could no longer trust him, either. How low had I sunk! Surely my daughters would hate her even more than the Beast! Oh, the things my subjects would say: while Louis XIV had settled down in his later years, I'd done the opposite! And yet, I'd also been deceived!

But it was too late: I needed her. Though I hadn't expected my sins to include a person of such low extraction, perhaps it didn't have to matter so much, when it was I who granted rank. While I dreaded the even worse ridicule that would instantly come, I'd been no stranger to it, either, when some even suspected that I'd had relations with my own daughter Adélaïde. As if I couldn't differentiate, or didn't have endless others lining up for their turn!

The more I considered Jeanne Bécu's life, the more a deepened sympathy tugged at my heart. What difficulties had pushed her to such a situation... even as it was becoming increasingly common. The more that I turned it over, it settled on the same thing: of her disarming affection and presence. Most importantly, she was nothing like the

Beast, for the simple fact that she seemed little interested in running my political affairs. And then, more than ever before, was the mangled satisfaction churning in my core: of scandalizing the court with my choices and reminding them who was the Absolute master.

Lebel died—perhaps as divine retribution—and Jeanne Bécu was given his quarters of six rooms in the wing of the Chapelle. She was hastily married, and her papers made of fictitious ancestors, since—in light of constant streams of entitled "nobles"—my edict of 1759 required providing proof of noble ancestry going back to 1400. I'd have to find someone to agree to present her to court, and though it might be some time, it would surely happen.

Some good news arrived with the return of Boungainville at the port of Saint-Malo, who was instantly hailed as a hero. Not only had he been the first Frenchman to sail around the world—all the way to Tahiti and the Samoan islands—but his crew of 340 had only suffered seven casualties. With a team including botanist Commerson, naval officer and explorer Lapérouse, and astronomer Veron, it was a welcomed bolster to our prestige after our defeat from the Seven Years' War.

At last an elderly countess was persuaded, thanks to a large sum, to present Jeanne Bécu at the nearly empty court. I tried not to think of what my departed son might've said—or done—had he been alive, while his sisters feigned smiles and the Dauphin seemed to grumble. He was approaching marriageable age too, and I suspected that, like his father, he would never have mistresses, and might in part resent the very idea because of me.

But the lightness of infatuation was too strong for me to resist, and time passed as I lavished her in gifts of jewelry, apartments, and the Château de Louveciennes, which would be a pleasant getaway from court. Nor did I care if the costs surpassed that which had been granted the Beast. Jeanne Bécu sat as Flora for a portrait by Drouais, and though I delighted for all to see it displayed at the Salon, it would never compare to that of Pauline Félicité by Nattier.

After four years of working and living among us in his quarters at Versailles, I granted Goldoni a pension, though lower than what we'd requested of the officials. It touched me that given our consecutive griefs he had not dared to say anything about compensation for a while. As his Italian tutoring position was no longer needed at court, I trusted we'd hear more of him as he stayed in touch and pursued his work in Paris.

Eager to show off our porcelain wares, I also liked to host annual displays in three new rooms, as much to reveal the latest products as to encourage our courtiers, ever wanting of new luxuries, to buy them.

I hoped that Louis XIV approved, as his idea came to fruition with the inauguration of l'Opéra Royale—that great uniting vessel of all the arts—built by Gabriel. First begun two years prior, it boasted of the largest concert hall in Europe.

Soon after, I was also pleased to meet Jacques Portefaix in Fontainbleau where, in the presence of Choiseul, I gave him a scholarship to continue his studies. Five years after his brave defense against the creature in Gévaudan, he was a tall seventeen-year-old with brown hair and a big nose, with a scar on one side of it. I looked into his large eyes, half hoping I'd see what he'd seen—the elusive fiend I still couldn't name. A wolf-dog hybrid? Or a hyena or some other exotic animal? I envied that he'd lived to fight it and tell the tale, when so many had been killed, and even some of my most skilled men had failed to come as close to it, let alone to catch it.

As Austrian Empress Maria Theresa favored strengthening our alliance, I requested the hand of Maria Antonia, her penultimate child, for my grandson the Dauphin. While I found it amusing that her nickname for her was Madame Antoine, she would be called Marie Antoinette when in France. To my further surprise, the Empress had even suggested her twenty-five-year-old daughter, Marie-Elisabeth as a wife for my widowed self, and while I didn't decline—especially if attractive—I wasn't in a hurry to remarry or distance myself from my mistress.

Soon after I realized there would be two weddings—one of which I hadn't expected. As we prepared to welcome the Dauphin's betrothed, Marie Antoinette, my youngest daughter Louise announced wanting to take the veil with the Carmelites at the convent of Saint-Denis. The banishment of the Jesuits, the death of her brother, her sister-in-law, her mother the Queen, and my latest mistress had all convened to finally convince her to take this fated step. I found it another cruel stab to my heart—yet how could I refuse? She was adamant of redeeming my soul and expiating my sins with her sacrifice, and even in my conflicted defiance and happiness I could not deny that I needed it. I almost suggested that since she'd taken to secretly wearing the religious dress while at Versailles, she could've just kept at it, but of course it wouldn't be the same.

The fifteen-year-old Louis Auguste and fourteen-year-old Marie Antoinette married in the royal chapel. Suspecting that he was more nervous than she was, I saw something familiar in his blushing and trembling as they exchanged rings. I wondered if my grandson saw her being born on the day after the devastating Lisbon earthquake as a much-needed sign of blessing or one of impending catastrophe.

I gifted the Dauphine a bronze-gilded ivory clock whose face I turned, and welcomed the opportunity to host another lavish affair to demonstrate the power of the French monarchy, even as I tried not to shed tears for missing the Queen and my son. Though likely to resemble his departed *dévot* father, Louis Auguste also shared my passion for hunting and joined me, Adélaïde, and Sophie in lathe turning objects. In part because of his own secretive, reclusive nature, it seemed all the more reason to make it a memorable affair, full of games and dazzling lights, and best of all, a marvelous feast in the new opera built by Gabriel.

Naturally, the celebration extended for days with shows and balls. But our rejoicing came to an abrupt end when a massive crowd gathered on Place Louis XV to watch the lightshow and fireworks. When one of them fell and set a scaffolding on fire, a panicked stampede ensued, leaving at least one hundred and thirty two bodies trampled to death, and others wounded.

If it hadn't already, it would've been said eventually: that there was the clear sign that my sins were being passed on to them. And while the upset Dauphin knew it was no compensation, he at least instantly showed his own caring nature by giving his full month's allowance to ease their suffering.

Despite their youth and shyness, I hoped that the young couple would find solace and refuge in each other's arms. I mused that the fruit of their endeavor might arrive sooner than the Queen and I with our twins, when Marie Antoinette's mother—that headstrong Empress Maria Theresa—had birthed no less than sixteen children. I mused that our new Dauphine might also like to join us on the hunt sometime.

Nostalgia flooded me once more, for better and worse. How different things might've been if the Queen hadn't shut her door to me... We might've had other sons... And I might've been more loyal to her and her memory if she'd died in the process. But what had her faith been if it couldn't sustain her through her duty? Or had she, in her own way, feared death more than duty? It couldn't be, as peacefully as she went... Such were the excuses I tried to make, for the worst was in the lingering sense that it wouldn't have changed the way I am. It still hurt to think that she simply hadn't wanted to keep going. And yet, I hadn't wanted to stop, either. And I dreaded most that, like an eternal pile of rotting carrion, I might never be able to.

At last, Corsica officially became a province of France, and in early fall we welcomed a new member to our menagerie, which was none other than a rhinoceros gifted to me by Jean-Baptiste Chevalier, the French governor to Chandernagor.

In part concerned that Jeanne Bécu's entourage might remain small, I also gave her a companion named Zamor from Bengal that the Duc de Richelieu had acquired from English slave traders. Rather than mere amusement fashionable at court, I thought he could serve as an unusual lesson in caring and motherhood for one such as herself. She soon had him baptized as Louis Benoit, dressed in a white ensemble braided with silver, and matching silver buttons, belt, and saber. It seemed she thought that increasingly referencing the Beast as her model might please me, when it had the opposite effect. I consoled myself with the hope that having Zamor around not only differed from her predecessor, but would keep her busier than her precious pet parrot or diamond-collared white greyhound, Mirza.

Other times I enjoyed visiting my mistress at Louveciennes and spending time with her away from court, as she showed me the new eastern wing, and decorations of carved woodwork that she had Gabriel implement, and an elegant neoclassical music pavilion by Ledoux.

Recently completed and never used by the Beast, I also enjoyed fine *soupers* at the Petit Trianon with Jeanne Bécu and some close friends. The neoclassical building had a simple square plan, decorated with woodwork motifs to honor nature.

With my enduring wish to bolster my image, I also contemplated Louis XIV's Grand Project dream of rebuilding the façades facing Paris. What seemed an extravagance given our lack of funds, I secretly welcomed financial help from none other than my mistress for Gabriel to undertake the Gabriel Wing.

Jeanne Bécu had succeeded in reviving me... But was that her talent or something much more evil? Not in her, in me... But was she adding her own, or soothing me? Both! It had to be both! Accept, refuse! Refuse, accept! I didn't want to think of those with whom she'd learned these intimate tricks—but sometimes I saw them, and all the worse in the act! It wasn't just our two tortured moans, but countless others—women and men. Some in masks, furs, even horns, smelling of lavender, bergamot, and musk, then urine and blood... Until there was something else; a too young hand...

I rolled off her, hoping the unreleased hard pain would give me the one climax that would finally do it: death! The only thing I deserved!

Or perhaps I was dead—I'd been dead all along, and I didn't even know it! It would explain why I'd so often sought something else, some escape—a remedy... to no avail! The pleasure always too brief for another nightmare to replace it; why had it taken me so long to realize that it didn't exist! No tricks of hers, or anyone else's, would ever succeed, much less when she echoed the Beast more and more—if I wanted she could be my perfect procuress... And though I would never say it, I wasn't sure how much more of it I could take.

And then, came another hint that I was far from being the only crazy or eccentric one. As if Charles-Geneviève hadn't done enough to be talked about, I heard a rumor of him actually being a woman. I chuckled, wondering what demon had possessed him now—then I retracted the thought, and even secretly apologized to him. No demon could have a hold on him, when there was simply no information on him having any tryst, with either woman or man!

Unless... A playful thrill seized me: did he know how to hide secrets better than anyone else from our age? Why hadn't I investigated when I had the chance! To think, I'd employed him for the *Secret du Roi*, and he might well be the secret himself—or curiously choose not to have many at all.

But I had to stop tormenting myself again on his account. Perhaps I would finally have him kidnapped and locked up, and order him to confess everything once and for all... He owed me that much as his king! But surely that was unnecessary, and better yet if someone else got to it first.

A likely overdue dismissal took place when Choiseul tried once more to bring us into war with Britain over the Falkland Islands. Since we'd given the Falkland Islands to Spain a few years prior, it was my decision to avoid more warfare and let them settle this matter—hopefully peaceably—of the Spanish capture of the British Port Egmont among themselves. Though the decision had been entirely mine, his departure also pleased his enemy Jeanne Bécu, when he'd remained bitter about my not ceding to the mistress of his choice, and his other intrigues. I had Maupeou take his place as prime minister.

I soothed and pleased myself by lathe turning an ivory clock made by watchmaker Jean-Antoine Lépine. Soon after, Boungainville's book on his adventures to Tahiti, along with descriptions of Argentina, Patagonia, and Indonesia also appeared to great acclaim. While I appreciated his achievement and enthusiasm for mankind, I didn't necessarily share his naïve Rousseau-esque views of the inherent goodness of man.

To support me in that view was Maupeou who did my will in handling the Parlement with an overdue iron scepter. I realized that I shouldn't have bent so much in the past, but this time I would not. Predictably, our enduring wish to levy taxes on the privileged classes once more displeased the Parlement, and Maupeou was only too pleased when they went on strike. Maupeou ordered them to resume their duties, and when nearly all judges refused, he exiled them to remote provinces and deprived them of their offices. To prove that this time they would not be called back as they'd been in the past, he established several regional courts to handle judicial matters. With all the conflicts I'd tried to avoid in my life, I hardly thought of myself as a despot monarch, but if the time had come for it, then so be it.

The Dauphin's fifteen-year-old brother, Louis Stanislas, married Marie Joséphine of Savoy, from the same region my mother had come from. With his obesity, I had my concerns about their consummation, just as it was known that after a year of marriage, the Dauphin and Marie Antoinette had yet to consummate their own union. My emotion always came back as I thought of my departed son, the marriage and life advice I couldn't, but still had wanted to try to give him, and his children... But I became a child myself at the mere thought, and concluded that it would happen in due time, as it had for the Queen and I. At least the Dauphin was not taken to spreading false rumors of his libido, though by contrast I suspected that in his pride and competition with the Dauphin, Louis Stanislas might.

While I rejoiced for the Dauphin to have a blue-grey-eyed Dauphine who brought her much-needed pure, youthful glow, I was fast tiring of all the court bickering she'd been dragged into. As had been the case when the Beast lived, Mesdames convinced Marie Antoinette not to acknowledge my mistress. With what I trusted was sound counsel from her mother Empress Maria Theresa, the charade eventually passed when the Dauphine finally addressed her publicly. I also found it amusing that her mother favored the recent pastel portrait done of the sixteen-year-old Dauphine in red hunting attire. Unsurprisingly, Jeanne Bécu began emulating her hunting dress to please me, but even she couldn't surpass the Dauphine's horsemanship and youthful beauty that still allowed her to pass for a distinguished young man.

Jeanne Bécu had a portrait done by Dagoty with Zamor serving her a cup of coffee, and another by Greuze, in which she appears simply dressed in a blue nightgown, without ornamentation, and her long hair hanging down to one side, as if caught in the midst of her nonexistent *toilette*. While her lack of rouge would scandalize the court, I appreciated its honest depiction of her extraction and natural beauty. It did her justice as a rendition, for she maintained a similar poised calm even in the face of mounting libels, such as the notorious *Gazetier cuirassé*. Published by a low-life Frenchman named Morande residing in London, he'd surely gone there to exploit their free speech laws to tarnish me in any way possible.

From the same city also raged gossip that the crowds were eagerly placing hefty bets on Charles-Geneviève's gender and, while amusing in a sense, I hoped was not a desperate—and potentially dangerous—attempt for more income. I deemed him too intelligent not to know that spirits could fly high when dealing with astronomical sums.

I liked to think that perhaps he was just being his natural bold and confident self, as I was feeling myself becoming as well. At least, that's what I hoped it was, for I liked the prospect of that better than me being incorrigible in my errors. I cannot explain what it is, other than this constant wish to escape, a constant hope for something better... So I had other mistresses in tandem with Jeanne Bécu.

What had changed? For a time she had been enough for me, but I'd often thought the same before, and yet it always ended. If only she would stop worshipping the Beast... They had the same first name, but even if they were the same person in different bodies—with the second far making up for the sensual disappointments of the first!—something in me swore that things would not be the same this time. Just as well, sometimes I knew Zamor and I had the same revengeful thought when we'd exchange a discreet glance while she'd tease him like a toy in front of her guests.

You're an untamed man; handle her how you want—I silently communicated to him, or perhaps it was he who whispered it to me.

Though I no longer saw la Belle Morphise, our three-year-old daughter Marguerite-Victoire having passed the fragile stage of early childhood, I happily made sure that she had a considerable pension for her care.

As for the arts, Goldoni dedicated his first French comedy play *Le Bourru bienfaisant* to my daughter Adélaïde, which we enjoyed and met with great success.

I also delighted in the auction of part of the disgraced Choiseul's furniture, some of which I purchased. I gladly gifted some pink and gold floral silk sofas to my dear friend Adélaïde de Bullioud, Comtesse de Séran, as part of refurbishing her husband's new Château de La Tour.

At last I sent Drouet to London to check up on Charles-Geneviève, to remind him not to leave London without my permission, and if possible, settle the question of his nature. Likewise he could continue his conversation with the Polish King Stanislas Poniatowski, who was offering my mischievous agent a potential, though for a proud Frenchman, unlikely new career.

In the summer, Austria, Prussia and Russia signed a treaty that partitioned Poland and would shrink its territory by nearly one-third.

Then, six years after she'd first wished it, the Queen's Convent was inaugurated with our daughters in attendance.

My own thrill at reclaiming power and standing in my convictions gave me the flair for unbridled expression. So I told the jewelers Boehmer and Bassenge of my wish for a diamond necklace that would outshine all others, to be given to Jeanne Bécu. Extravagant, surely, and to speak the language of my greediest subjects, another clear reminder of my power.

In spring I commissioned Bachelier for a sixth painting of deer antlers. Set on a light blue background, it shows two nearly even antlers without tines; like blunted horns, two handless arms up, or just an unusual kind of horseshoe. Thus my private collection of bizarre antler paintings reached twelve, with six from Oudry and six from Bachelier.

As if on cue, I soon got word of Morande's threats to publish *The Secret Memoirs of a Public Woman*, a new licentious *libelle* targeting Jeanne Bécu... That some would say I had brought this on myself did not make it any less frustrating. On the one hand, I didn't care; things had always been said and would always be said about myself and whatever I did. But on the other, why not eliminate this vile work if it was a simple matter of the right price? Though I didn't expect it to be easy, not everyone was as unbending as Charles-Geneviève—whose true nature was still unconfirmed, and mattered little to me. So off I sent some agents to gather information and begin some negotiations to have this stopped, before it, and all the affairs of the *Secret du Roi* burst into the public. Though I would always have a lingering pride for this endeavor, that it hadn't yielded as much of the desired results, and worse, could be ridiculed because of me, was yet another bitter mark of my failure.

In the meantime I amused myself with yet another addition to our menagerie: an elephant, also gifted by the French governor to Chandernagor. Though she pleased me greatly, she had an unpredictable character that could be as friendly as mean. That she would so quickly reflect the bulk of the personalities at court made me appreciate her all the more.

Soon after I also rejoiced to have my youngest grandson, the handsome Charles Philippe, Comte d'Artois, and brother to the Dauphin, married to Marie Thérèse of Savoy. Thus she was rejoining her older sister Marie Joséphine at court, who'd married Louis Stanislas two years before. To think of all my grandchildren finally matched brought a much-needed sense of relief, no matter how temporary.

It was a frigid winter of January of '74 when we gave a ball at Versailles for the Dauphine. If I had a choice, I preferred to think that it was my age that was making me more sensitive, rather than the seasons were getting harsher. My poor yet tenacious subjects! Though they might hate me, I loved them still, and wanted only to embrace them all, if only I could—if only I was allowed… Though they'd come to doubt my sacred, healing touch, as I always had my own, I prayed it wasn't too late for the Dauphin. He was my heir, but he was also his own person, and his actions would prove it.

As the lights twinkled and the music blared, my head spun with *vin de Champagne*, but also something much more powerful.

Memories—of the hunts, of the Queen, of the birth of my twins, my Dauphin, my daughters, Pauline Félicité at the masked ball… and everything else by turns increasingly unfulfilling, bitter, or mediocre from there. Oh, to be young and pure again! It was so long ago that it almost seemed like I'd never been among them.

Thankfully, in the whirl I smiled at the thought of my most recent portrait underway by the innovative Vincent de Montpetit, using his new eludoric painting technique. I could already imagine the effect as my oil-and-water image would display on the glass surface. Dressed simply in crimson, with the blue sash of the Order of the Holy Spirit, I face viewers from my right side, my sad eyes contrasting my proud bearing and tentative smile.

I sniffled, the music gradually shifting to Vivaldi's "Spring" segment, played by an invisible—or even secret—orchestra…

*Did you think it would be that easy!*

It is pitch dark when I awake alone, and though I can see nothing, something tells me I'm in the Clock Room. My age, my memory... Had I been coming without remembering? Or worse, walking in my sleep?

*Hesitating again! Yet here I am, as you've always wanted!*

I freeze when the animated Passemant clock suddenly pounces wildly towards me, the planets spinning so fast in his planisphere glass head that they might shoot at me like bullets and canons. Though he has no arms, I'm suddenly aware that he can self-generate some and take me away at any moment.

Is it—time? I swallow. But why does it have to be—in that form, I say, on the verge of tears. Not this one that I so liked to watch change every new year!

*Well; if you insist on another. There is no shortage of options.*

The icy chuckle pierces me, and I don't have to look up to know that it's the Beast. No, please, not her, I say.

*What about that, then? A nice whip of discipline!*

Berryer. Not him either, please.

*Then certainly, him!*

More chuckles, friendlier. King George II and the III. The ones I lost so much to. Please, no. Anywhere but with them...

*Anywhere, no! For there, all your secrets are out, and there are no masks! So what will you do there?*

I stare in shock as the form morphs into a massive stag with antlers so large and sharp they could impale and slice me in one thrust.

Better! I sob, as the cackling laugher fuels my certainty that my desperation is only beginning.

*Better—You don't know what that is!*

Yes, I do! Please, believe me!

*Why should I believe you now, when each time the harm passes, you're worse than before! Clearly you've chosen to be a demon!*

I want to scream, say all I've ever wanted to say—but my lips are sealed. Worst of all, my sadness is deeper than I've ever known—and not even a glimpse of what's to come! How—I wish I could just break through it!

*Don't you know! Your hesitation was your warning—your conscience! If your eye causes you to sin! Where shall we start then!*

Damien! I shout, knowing I deserve as little pity as I showed him.

*Yes, all the way! Where shall we start then! Shoulder or leg! Scalping or castration! Torn neck or disembowelment! Or perhaps a slow starvation!*

Damien!—I sob once more the name I rarely uttered, as the stag is now breathing down my neck.

*Is it Damien who saves!*

No, but I'm—too ashamed to say His name. I need—I'd like to learn from him, from his strength... Is it allowed? Can I ever be forgiven?

*Even if it requires the same treatment!*

Yes! My torso rocks as I cry like a child, and I don't dare to look up, when I've made yet another vain request from the one who should least want to see or intercede for me.

The stag's breath burns my skin, and just when I think I'm slowly being incinerated, it vanishes. For a moment all is so still that I think I'm being taken somewhere without my knowledge. At last, the end has come, and like so many times before I didn't prepare, didn't do enough... But miraculously, I'm relieved that I deserve whatever comes, and that I might finally change for the better.

*What doesn't serve Him must be shed! Better sooner than later!*

Yes—I nod in the pitch darkness filled with only that palpable mighty voice.

*Do you submit to His will then!*

I do.

*Are you sure? Perhaps you have something better in mind?*

I'm sure that I don't.

*In that case: Comte de Lauraguais and Caron de Beaumarchais will resolve the libelle situation. Then the Secret du Roi will be exposed, and you will go to the Trianon and get the smallpox, that will add to your already loathsome Saturnian-leper reputation. You'll be buried hastily, with few in attendance and limited mourning. What do you say?*

Only...

*Well?*

That I thought I already had it?

*The fear of the Lord!*


My eyes open with a start, the quill still in my hand as I sit in the Dispatch Room lit by a single short candle on the verge of burning out. I'm not sure how or when I ended up here, but my vision wells up as I hear the faint echo of "Spring," filling me with a sense of cozy relief. The fear of the Lord is the beginning of wisdom and knowledge. Nothing happens without Him. For the first time, something like unwavering certainty.

I put away my writing materials, no longer worried about this text being found, and if amusingly so, who will read and spread it. I even chuckle as I stack and wrap the papers, for who's to say "I" even wrote this, when it hardly feels like myself?

There are others, and surely my English-speaking son first among them who nudged me, and I will thank him for that, too. Perhaps it's best for it be unknown, or ignored, dissolved and vanished like so much else I tried to do. And though I often failed, I am grateful—and unworthy—to have been given the chance.

At last, the bitter cold is receding, and I'm ready for a few more walks in the earthly gardens, and into the place where reigns the One king who faultlessly bore men's crown of thorns.

# ACKNOWLEDGMENTS

This story was a reminder to me of how, after years of learning about 18<sup>th</sup> century France, a historical monarch I increasingly disliked could still catch me by surprise.

I'm grateful for the two main—and very different—biographic titles that have inspired my own approach to the elusive king. These French titles are Jean Christian Petitfils's *Louis XV* and Maurice Lever's *Louis XV, libertin malgré lui*. Other French sources include: the memoirs of Luynes and Comte Gabriel Mareschal de Bièvre, Arlette Farge's work, and Anne Muratori-Philip's biography on the too-often forgotten wife of Louis XV, *Marie Leszczynska*. Likewise, on the libertinism/hedonism that swept over the elites in that time, Patrick Wald Lasowski's *L'Amour au temps des libertins* makes for great reference. Though I haven't been able to read her work, I'm also grateful for Marion Sigaut, whose dedicated work I first learned about via YouTube years ago, on the often unreliable Voltaire.

Some equally rewarding English-language sources include: Julia V. Douthwaite, Catherine Girard, Richard N. Ellis and Charlie R. Steen, Robert Darnton, F. Hamilton Hazlehurst, John D. Woodbridge, and Kevin L. Justus. As a Christian with interest in the works of Swedenborg, I'm also grateful for his entry on the spiritual exchange between Louis XIV and Louis XV on the Bull *Unigenitus* on December 13, 1759; on which see his *Supplements*, §60.

To close with a note on the fascinating case of Gévaudan: growing up in 80s/90s Brussels, I recall hearing about wolf attacks in the countryside and some references to this 18<sup>th</sup> century event. Then, as now, I was confident that the creature was not local, and for a while the hyena seemed to me the likely contender. However, I've since gladly found what I believe to be the overdue answer in German biologist Karl-Hans Taake's *The Gévaudan Tragedy: The Disastrous Campaign of a Deported 'Beast'*.

# ABOUT THE AUTHOR

Born in Brussels, Belgium, Natacha Pavlov is a bilingual Christian writer of German, Russian, and Christian Palestinian heritage. A life-long book and storytelling enthusiast, her novel *Jayida* (2023) is the fruit of years of research and the project that first made her want to write historical fiction. She is also the author of the novella *Nicola's Leg* (2017) and the short story collection *Twisted Reflections* (2015).

She is currently at work on more historical fiction.

Visit her at www.natachapavlov.com.

www.ingramcontent.com/pod-product-compliance
Lightning Source LLC
Chambersburg PA
CBHW032251070726

47590CB00016B/2431